Fern

The Montgomery Sisters #1

KAT FLANNERY

FERN: THE MONTGOMERY SISTERS #1

Copyright © 2018 by Kat Flannery. All Rights Reserved.

No part of this publication may be reproduced, stored in a retrieval system, or transmitted, in any form or by any means, electronic, mechanical, photocopying, recording, or otherwise, without prior written permission from the author.

This is a work of fiction. Names, characters, places and incidents either are the product of the author's imagination or are used fictitiously. And any resemblance to actual persons, living, dead (or in any other form), business establishments, events, or locales is entirely coincidental.

www.katflannerybooks.com

SECOND EDITION Paperback

April 4, 2018

ISBN: 978-0-9811056-3-5

Cover designed by Carpe Librum Book Design

Novels by Kat Flannery

Chasing Clovers

The Branded Trilogy
Lakota Honor (Book 1)
Blood Curse (Book 2)
Sacred Legacy (Book 3)

Hazardous Unions:
Two Tales of a Civil War Christmas
(*by Alison Bruce & Kat Flannery*)

The Montgomery Sisters Trilogy
FERN (Book 1**)**
POPPY (Book 2)

Fern

"Gratitude is the fairest blossom which springs from the soul."

~Henry Ward Beecher

Chapter One

Wyoming Territory, 1880

Fern Montgomery was desperate. She slapped the reins onto Nelly's brown back.

"Faster! Faster!"

The old mare couldn't go any quicker. The horse was all she had. A lack of money and other necessities were a priority. A Thoroughbred hadn't been in the budget, but at this very moment a stallion was what she wished for.

She snapped the reins again. "Damn it, Nelly. Get going."

She didn't like to swear. Her younger sister did plenty of it for both of them, but today she'd make an exception. She glanced behind her at the woman lying beaten in the back of the wagon. Sarah Fuller had come to her on more than one occasion. Fern had used the remedies taught to her by her father to mend the cuts and bruises Sarah's husband, Robby, had given her.

Today was different. Sarah had arrived slumped over her horse and unconscious, her face so badly bruised and swollen she was almost unrecognizable. But when Fern tried to wake her there was no response. Without a second thought she'd left her sisters and headed into town.

She needed to get Sarah to Doc Miller's. There was something wrong beyond Fern's abilities, and she wasn't qualified to assess her to determine what it was. She knew her plants and the vegetables within her garden well. She also knew how to use them medicinally. Her father, a doctor, had believed in using the landscape and what it grew in aiding the sick. Not everything could be cured with opium or morphine, he'd say. When he passed away two years ago, Fern had continued to help those who came to her. It was her passion and how she supported her younger sisters. She loved toiling in the soil, caring for her plants, and she enjoyed helping those in need.

She pulled on the reins to slow Nelly down as the wagon rounded a corner on the dirt road. The sun was climbing higher in the sky, and she wiped a bead of sweat from her brow as she passed the creek. Had there been time she would've stopped to soak her handkerchief and lay it at the base of her neck to cool her off. Instead her heart thumped rapidly in her chest causing her face to flush. Tiny black dots danced before her eyes. She blinked to clear her vision. She fanned her face and slapped the reins with the other hand. *Please God, let Sarah be okay.*

She blew out a long sigh when she saw the church on the outskirts of town.

"Almost there, Sarah," she whispered more for herself than her unconscious friend.

Main Street was busy with women and children shuffling along the boardwalk. Men lined up outside the livery waiting for supplies while several elderly men puffed on their pipes a few feet away.

She passed Mayor Smith standing in front of his office. She shivered. He repulsed her. Refusing to meet his glare, she stared straight ahead. The rotund man wanted Fern for his wife. After many polite declines he turned bitter, siding with Pete Miller in his charge to stop her from selling the natural medicine. There was no way she'd agree to such an absurd demand, and her choice resulted in a one-sided feud with the two men doing everything in their power to stop her.

She pulled on the reins and halted the wagon in

front of the doctor's office. She hiked up her skirt and jumped from the seat. There was no time for etiquette. She was sure the uppity women of Manchester were tipping their noses at her now. Well she didn't care. If any one of them came near her, she'd blast them.

Fern pulled on the door and nearly took her arm off. It was locked.

"Doc's gone to lunch," a deep voice said from behind her. "Can I help you with something?"

"Not unless you're a doctor," she replied, ignoring him to climb into the back of the wagon and assess her friend.

"What happened to her?"

"She showed up at my place beaten and unconscious."

He jumped into the back of the wagon. She had no choice but to acknowledge him then. Wide shoulders fitted within a denim shirt displayed thick arms and a wide chest. Her gaze moved upward to a square jaw, high cheekbones and dark brown eyes. A jagged scar cut up the left side of his face to pull the corner of his eye down just a bit. It looked to be from a knife, but she couldn't say for sure.

He coughed.

Her cheeks grew warm, and she focused on her friend.

Brows furrowed, he inspected Sarah's arms, legs and back.

"Why did she come to your place?"

"She visited often."

He brushed the hair from Sarah's face and inhaled sharply.

"What the hell?"

"She's been beaten. I told you that."

"Did you do this?"

"Of course not."

His eyes locked with hers.

"Do I look like I could do something like this? She was my friend."

He shrugged.

She bit down hard on her bottom lip to stop herself from going off on the oaf.

"How long has she been in your care?"

"Half an hour. The length of time it took me to get here."

He placed two fingers to her neck.

"Why?"

"Because she's dead."

"She can't be. I checked her pulse before we left my place."

Fern looked down at her friend and nudged her shoulder.

"Sarah. Sarah, wake up."

The girl's wheat colored hair fell across her face, and Fern watched for a faint movement, a waving strand from her breath, anything to hint there was life. There was nothing. No even rise and fall of her chest. No pink cheeks. She reached for her hand; it was cold and limp within her own. She brushed the hair from Sarah's swollen face and knew she was gone. A sob slipped from her lips as she leaned down to wrap Sarah in her arms and hold her.

"I'm so sorry," she whispered past her tears. It wasn't fair. She was so young, so full of life and she was taken so tragically. She'd been dealt horror after horror at the hands of her bastard of a husband. Fern squeezed her tighter, pulling every memory from their short friendship closer to her. The poor thing never had a chance to live.

"Why didn't you listen to me? Why didn't you leave?"

"Ma'am?"

Fern pressed herself away from Sarah and wiped her eyes. She'd forgotten he was there.

He was staring at her, his dark gaze scrutinizing.

"I need to ask you some questions," he said again.

"I don't have time. I need to find the sheriff." She moved toward the back of the wagon.

"I am the sheriff."

That explained his inquisitive nature.

"Where is Sheriff Bell?"

"He took a job down in Texas a few months ago."

Had it been that long since she'd been to town?

"Gabe Bennett." He tipped his Stetson. "We need to talk."

She nodded, followed him out of the wagon and onto the street.

"What about—"

"Arrest that woman," Pete Miller shouted from the street.

Oh boy.

Doctor Miller walked toward them, his tall lean frame dressed in tanned slacks and a cotton dress shirt with the top two buttons undone. He was handsome and he knew it.

"What have you done now, Miss Montgomery?"

"You want me arrested, yet you know nothing of why I am here," Fern said.

"I presume it is because of the woman in the back of your wagon."

"That woman is my friend, Sarah Fuller."

"And she's dead," Sheriff Bennett added.

She pressed her lips firmly together.

Pete turned narrowed eyes toward her.

"You've done it now, Miss Montgomery. I knew all along you were an imposter pretending to help the innocent people of Manchester with your elixirs."

"I've done no such thing and you know it. I am not responsible for Sarah's death," Fern said matter-of-factly.

"We shall see. After all, I am the one with the degree in medicine."

"My father had a degree in medicine too, but also knew the benefits from using what the earth grew to help those who were ill."

"Doctor Montgomery is dead."

She flinched.

"He should've stuck to the use of opium and what he studied in school instead of teaching you about such rubbish as herbs and plants."

"He was a good doctor. The people of Manchester adored him. He saved many lives."

"He also lost some."

She didn't miss the ominous look flash within his eyes.

"You and I both know some things cannot be controlled."

He came close, leaning into her side.

"Unless you want me to tell the good people of Manchester about Adam Montgomery and his *skills*, I suggest you keep quiet," he whispered.

"What are you talking about?"

"I'm sure they'd be interested to know why a doctor of such high prestige, sought after even, would leave a prospering practice in Boston to come to Manchester, Wyoming."

Fern ran her back teeth together and met his sinister gaze with a glare of her own. How he'd known of the accident surprised her, but she refused to let him see that.

"I hardly see how it will do any good. My father has been passed for almost two years. His reputation will stand by whatever rubbish you spout."

He smiled.

"Ahh, but will yours?"

She had nothing else to say to him. She loved her work and even more so loved helping those in need. He'd found out secrets, ones better left buried with her father. She refused to push him further. If the people of Manchester took him at his word, she'd have no more clients—which meant no income and means to support her sisters.

"Good girl." He smiled and motioned to two men. "Carry the deceased inside."

"She has a name."

He gave her a sideways glance.

"Sarah Fuller. You should know that."

"Should I?"

"Yes," she growled.

He leaned over to take a look at Sarah.

"She does seem familiar, but I see so many patients it's hard to keep track."

He was a liar. Manchester had a population of a little over a thousand, including the farmers on the outskirts of the town. Her father knew every patient's name. Doctor Miller irked her, and she wished for half the brass her sister, Poppy, had so she could slug him.

"Now, kindly move aside," he said.

She stepped back and allowed them to take her friend. All eyes were on her, and she wanted nothing more than to go home. She didn't fit in here. She wasn't her father. She wasn't a man.

A few of the women who used her roots and herbs sent her shy smiles of reassurance, while their husbands glared at her. Lucy Miller grasped Fern's hand, giving it a light squeeze before she followed her husband into his office. The doctor's wife was a kind woman who never used Fern's herbs, but didn't judge her either. Once the door closed to Doctor Miller's office, she decided to take her leave as well.

"Miss Montgomery, I need to speak with you."

"Robby Fuller. He killed her." She was tired, hungry and devastated.

"How can you be so sure?"

"Because Sarah was my friend. I'd given her witch hazel many times to help with the bruises and swelling he'd left on her body."

"I am assuming her husband used his hands on her often?"

"Sadly, yes."

"But that doesn't mean he killed her."

She spun around to face him. Anger filled her body and spilled from her lips.

"Of course he killed her. Anyone who'd beat a woman as badly as he did is capable of murdering them."

He crossed his arms, and the sun glinted off the silver star pinned to his chest. She wondered why she hadn't noticed it before.

"True, but you cannot rule out all possibilities."

"There are no other possibilities, *Sheriff*."

"There is one."

"What is that?"

"You."

Gabe paid close attention to her reaction. Her face turned a bright shade of red, blue eyes burst into flames and she pulled her lips into a tight smile. He'd riled her, which is what he'd intended. Most people confessed or said something out of turn when they lost their temper, and he was hoping she'd do the same.

"What kind of elixirs do you sell?"

She lifted her chin.

"You're a medicine woman?"

"Some would say so. I chose to be called a gardener."

"I don't give a damn what you are. Do you give herbs and other homemade elements to the sick or injured?"

"Yes."

"Then you are a suspect."

She locked her eyes with his in a stealthy glare.

"Sarah was not poisoned. She was beaten to death."

"I never said anything about poison, but now that you've mentioned it I will need to investigate that notion."

"You've got to be joking."

"Wish I was, but the sad fact is that Mrs. Fuller was murdered, and someone did it."

"Yes, her blasted husband!"

"Seems to be the logical answer, but I need to rule out everything."

"Very well, until you have some evidence, which I am sure you won't, I am going home."

"I'll be seeing you soon."

"Don't count on that," she called over her shoulder before climbing into the seat of the wagon.

He'd heard many things about Fern Montgomery and wondered if any of them were true. Was that little bit of a female capable of killing her friend?

Chapter Two

Fern unharnessed Nelly and led her into the stall before pulling the rope over the gate to fasten it closed. She scooped a handful of oats and gave them to the mare.

"Good girl."

The small barn needed repairs. The walls were rotting, the wood broken and split. There had been no extra money to fix things properly. She'd enlisted her sisters to nail up the boards as best they could. It looked terrible, but it kept the coyotes and other animals out.

She went to the small table to inspect her seedlings. She'd started most of her plants within the barn, and as they matured she transplanted them outside or moved them to the garden room off of the cabin. The small room her father built before he passed had a glass roof that let the sun in and helped her plants flourish, especially in the colder months.

She fingered a tiny stem of rosemary and released a long breath, still unable to believe Sarah was gone. She was Fern's age and over the last few months they'd become friends. She begged her to leave Robby countless times, but Sarah loved him, an emotion Fern didn't think she'd ever get to experience. Men out west expected a lot from their spouses, and she'd seen the effects their rough treatment had on them. She wasn't sure she'd ever find a man who would understand her love of plants. Most saw it as a gross waste of time, when instead she should be having babies or working in the fields until her fingers bled.

She wasn't afraid of hard work, she'd done her fair share on their homestead, but she'd die a spinster before she'd allow a man to dictate her every move. She'd held onto her beliefs, and because of them, it was mostly women who came to see her to ask for advice on menstruating, pregnancy and any other ailment they had. A handful of men used her remedies, but on strict instruction she was to keep the business to herself.

She thought of Sheriff Bennett, and her stomach twisted. How dare he accuse her of killing Sarah?

Poisoning her even! If he had half a brain in his head he'd see it was that spineless Robby Fuller who'd done her in. She straightened, refusing to think of the arrogant lawman anymore, and left the barn to check on her garden.

The afternoon sun was stifling and the air was heavy. She could feel her body heating underneath the cotton dress.

Row upon row of vegetables and herbs grew in her yard. She knew where everything was and what they were used for. There were many days she'd kept solace within the dirt and the greenery she'd learned to love. It gave her peace, a sense of belonging she hadn't found within Manchester and with some of the town folk there.

She sighed. It was just as well. She was different, and she'd not compromise herself for anyone.

She stopped at the first row and stared at the trampled beets. Jaw clenched, hands fisted, she held back the string of curses she wanted to bellow. *Poppy.* Her sister was going to be the death of her yet. A bead of sweat slid down her forehead, and she flexed her shoulders to loosen the damp dress that clung to her overheated skin. Letting out an exhausted breath, she ran a hand across her face and knelt down to inspect the damaged leaves.

Footprints were still visible within the soft soil. Fern growled as she dug into the dirt to pull a flattened beet from the earth. It was split in two. She threw the soil and dug another. It was wrecked as well.

She headed for the small cabin nestled against a stand of oak and pine trees. Damp tendrils of hair clung to the sides of her face. What she wouldn't give for a cool breeze right now. Shoulders set, she readied herself to face her abrasive sister. The door to the cabin swung open, and a flash of red hair bolted from the door.

"How is Sarah?" Poppy asked.

Her anger dissolved with Poppy's question. Tears sprang in her eyes, and she blinked them away. "She's gone."

"That rotten son of a bitch." Her sister stomped her booted foot. The girl hated dresses, and much to Fern's disapproval wore pants and a cotton shirt instead.

"Poppy, must you use such words?"

"I could use others, but you'd not approve of them either."

"Try to speak like a young lady and not a cowboy in from the fields."

"I ought to go on over to the Fuller place and put a bullet in that yellow-bellied bastard."

"That will not solve anything."

"Yes it will! He'll get what he deserves for treating poor Sarah the way he did."

She couldn't argue with her sister; the girl was right. She'd love to see Robby Fuller beaten bloody the way he did to her friend.

"We have enough trouble with the doc and half of Manchester. We don't need anymore."

The girl shrugged and walked away.

"Stop," Fern commanded, remembering her garden and the ruined beets.

Poppy halted and swiveled to aim angry blue eyes toward her.

"Where do you think you're going?"

"If I can't go knock some sense into that sissy, Robby, I'm headin' to the hills to check my traps."

"You're not going anywhere until you fix what you've done to my garden."

The girl stood on her tiptoes and turned toward the garden.

"All is well. I see nothin' that needs fixin'."

Just like her to try and weasel out of what she'd done. The girl lived in those blasted hills doing goodness knows what half the day.

"It isn't. Look again."

She blew out a long sigh that tossed the white

string of hair from her forehead. Poppy had been born with rich auburn hair most girls would envy. It was the streak of white that when her hair was parted hung to the right an inch wide they didn't want, and was the brunt of most of their teasing when she was little. Pa had said it was a birthmark that caused the hair to turn snow white, but Fern believed it was a gift. On days when Poppy had been ridiculed at school by the other kids, Fern had comforted her by telling her she was special, different, and to cherish the bold ribbon of hair as a testament to how unique she was. Now, with the girl just past sixteen, she feared it held more meaning and played a vital part in making her sister the brassy hellcat she was today.

"I looked and saw nothin' of what you said has been done."

"Poppy, you've trampled my beets."

She shook her head.

"Yes, you did."

"Must you always accuse me of being the culprit when things go wrong?"

Her statement was true but in Fern's defense it was always Poppy doing the damage.

"Who else?"

"Ivy?"

Their younger sister could've been the one, but she

was inside sleeping off the bad headache she'd had the night before.

"She is sick."

Poppy shrugged.

Fern crossed her arms, determined to make her sister admit to what she'd done.

"Fix it."

"I will not."

"Poppy Montgomery, you will mend that row of beets or else."

A horse neighed from the bushes behind the cabin. Before Fern could say another word Poppy pulled her Colt from the holster around her waist and pointed the gun at Sheriff Bennett as he came into view.

He pulled on the reins to stop his horse and relaxed his arms, one over the other, in front of him.

"State your damn business," Poppy yelled.

"Poppy, put down the gun," Fern said.

"Not until the bastard states his business."

"That bastard is the sheriff," she whispered between clenched teeth.

"Let me see your star."

"I'm going to need to reach inside my pocket. You're not going to shoot me are you?"

"Do I look like a Nancy boy? I ain't gonna shoot

you, just do as you're told and show me the damn star."

"Bossy little thing aren't you?" He pulled the silver star from his pocket and held it so they could see it. "Satisfied?"

Poppy holstered her gun.

He dismounted and walked toward them.

"Miss Montgomery." He tipped his head, the brown Stetson shading his eyes from the sun and her view.

"What are you doing here?" she asked, irritated from her fight with Poppy and his unexpected visit.

"I thought I'd come by to finish our conversation and have a look at what the doc is chirpin' about back in town."

"Pete Miller doesn't have a lick of sense in his bull head," Poppy chimed in.

"And who might you be?" he asked.

"None of your damn business."

"You aimed your Colt on me, I'd say I have a right to know," he said.

"Poppy," Fern warned, before she turned toward him. "My sister."

"You allow her to wear pants?"

"I am my own person, Sheriff. I wear what I want."

"I can see that." He assessed Poppy before training his dark gaze onto her. "Can she shoot that thing, or is it just for show?"

Poppy pulled her Colt, spun the chamber and fired, knocking two glass bottles from the fence twenty yards away.

"Son of a bitch," he said.

"I can shoot anything."

He looked at Fern.

"It's true. Poppy's skills with the weapon are remarkable."

"Can you shoot a moving target?" he asked.

She took his hat from on top of his head, threw it into the air, pulled her Colt and shot a hole right through the Stetson.

"That's my bloody hat! You ruined my damn hat." He stomped toward the Stetson, now lying on the ground, picked it up and put his finger through the hole. "Ah, hell."

"You may go now, Poppy," Fern said, hoping her sister took the hint and skedaddled before Sheriff Bennett lost his temper.

"I ain't going nowhere."

"You're not. The proper word is *not*, Poppy."

Her sister rolled her eyes. Fern wanted to crawl back to bed and forget this day ever happened.

"Is it just the two of you on the homestead?" he asked, scanning the yard around them, his hat crumpled in his hand.

"We have another sister, Ivy, she's twelve," Fern answered.

"Is she like that one?" He pointed to Poppy.

"Bootlicker."

Fern grabbed her sister's arm, having had enough of her antics, and escorted her to the front door of the cabin.

"Get inside before you get me arrested," she whispered.

"Fine, but if you need me just holler." She leaned around Fern to stick her tongue out at Sheriff Bennett.

"Damn it, get!" She shoved the wild girl through the door and slammed it shut.

"There is a nice boarding school just past Cheyenne."

"Do not tell me how to raise my sisters, Sheriff."

"Was just offering some advice is all."

"I don't need your advice. Now, why have you come?"

Chapter Three

Gabe had never met a woman so abrupt, especially one who should be looking for a husband instead of living a spinster's life. With that kind of attitude she'd never find a man and neither would her foul-mouthed, gun-toting sister.

"I came to talk to you."

"What is it you want to discuss?" She let out the words in a long sigh, and he assessed her appearance for the first time. The skin around her eyes creased, and the lines in her forehead crinkled together as she frowned. He'd bet under different circumstances she'd be a beauty, but the messed braid, worn clothes, and sun-kissed skin placed her in an unnatural element—one he was not comfortable being in. She looked different from all the women he'd come across. Most were demure and dainty; she was none of those things. She was foreign to everything he'd known or had ever seen, and within the blue depths of her eyes…he saw life.

He scowled.

He'd come for information, not to get mooneyes over the girl, damn it. He had a job to do. Pete Miller was determined Fern was the one responsible for killing Mrs. Fuller, but Gabe had his doubts. The woman had been beaten, which seemed to be the obvious cause of her demise, not some elixir sold to her by the tiny herb collector.

It was clear Pete didn't like his business going to a woman, one without an education or degree no less. Gabe made it his business to find out more about Fern Montgomery and what secrets she had.

"I'd like to know how often Mrs. Fuller visited you," he asked.

She walked toward the porch and leaned against the railing. The shoddy fence bent awkwardly as she placed her weight on it.

"Sarah and Robby moved here last year from Colorado. She started coming to see me when she couldn't get pregnant. I gave her some winter cherry to help with her immune system, but we didn't know if it was her that could not conceive or Robby who couldn't release his seed."

He cleared his throat. She was blunt and to the point, a mannerism he was neither familiar nor comfortable with.

"The wild cherry didn't work, so I gave her echinacea root. That did not work either."

"It was the husband."

She nodded.

"When did you notice Sarah showing up with bruises?"

"Almost immediately after I'd gotten to know her. I think she always had them, but hid the marks under long sleeves, shawls and bonnets. Once she got to know me, her trust grew, and she wasn't afraid to show me. The pain was unbearable sometimes. She knew I could help her with it."

"And I assume you did."

"Yes. We used all sorts of rubs, teas and smoke."

"Smoke?"

"It is a plant, or root that is burned within a small area. You breathe in the smoke. It is very effective."

"But not for Mrs. Fuller."

"Her bruises were one on top of the other. They never healed before he'd give her a new one. Three months ago Robby broke her arm."

"You mended it?"

"No, I sent her to Doc Miller."

"Good thinking."

"One would assume. Instead it raised all sorts of trouble."

"Like what?"

"Pete has had it out for me for a long while. He and Mayor Smith needed a reason to push me out of town and this seemed to be it."

"How so?"

"Robby Fuller came to call."

Gabe didn't like where this was going.

"I wasn't expecting him and therefore wasn't prepared. Thank goodness for Poppy. That girl can wield a gun like an outlaw."

"So I've seen. What did Robby do?"

She closed her eyes. When she opened them, he saw determination and resilience—two traits he admired.

"Trampled most of my garden. Tried to burn down the cabin, but Poppy held him off. I reckon he'll come by here soon enough to retaliate for Sarah. Pete will put him up to it."

Gabe's hands fisted, and he clenched his jaw. Three females, one a little girl, out here in the middle of nowhere, defenseless to whatever came their way.

"I'll speak to the doc."

"Won't do you any good."

"I can be persuasive."

"You will lose your job. Mayor Smith won't hold to you taking my side."

"I'm not on anyone's side."

She turned from him to gaze at the bountiful garden before them.

"You'd mentioned your father while we were in town."

"Yes."

"He was a doctor?"

She nodded.

"He served the people of Manchester for three years before he died a few years ago."

"What made them turn on you?"

"Pa always used the plants within his practice. Some patients were deathly against it while others approved. But he was a doctor. I am not."

"If you were a doctor they'd accept your way of doing things?"

"Maybe, but I think the problem lies much deeper than that."

"I'm not sure I understand."

"I am a woman."

Pete Miller felt threatened by this tiny female? He almost burst out laughing the thought was so absurd. She was smart, he didn't doubt that. He was fully aware she knew how and what each plant's medicinal use was, but a threat? Not a chance. Her knowledge of the shrubs placed her in a tricky spot. She could've given something to Mrs. Fuller by accident, or on purpose. He didn't trust her enough to wipe her slate clean just yet. He was determined to get to know her before that happened.

He'd speak with Pete to see if he'd found out the cause of death yet. He wasn't sure why he hoped Fern wasn't involved, but he didn't like the feeling and brushed the nostalgia away. His job came first before any harebrained emotions his lower half might have.

Chapter Four

Gabe grabbed his new Stetson from the desk and planted it firmly on top of his head. He missed his old hat. The felt had been worked in and molded to his head perfectly.

Both of his cells were occupied, and he hoped to have them emptied when the judge came through. The man was expected any day now. A loud snore echoed from the bunk on the left. Ralph Palmer was sleeping off all of the whiskey he'd consumed last night at the saloon, and would have to face the judge on all the damage he'd caused there.

Tommy Rainer, a bank robber, was in the other cell, putting Gabe on high alert. Tommy's gang had a reputation for busting their leader out of jail. The notorious Rainer gang had robbed eight banks in

Montana and Wyoming alone. The sooner he got rid of Tommy the less trouble would likely come his way.

He appointed retired Texas Ranger, Bill Holt, to help out while he continued with the other aspects of the job. Now with the murder of Mrs. Fuller he was thankful he had the other lawman at his side.

The old man was a quick draw with a keen sense of danger and his surroundings. His abilities and experience were welcome assets as well. When Gabe mentioned he might need help, the old man offered his time without hesitation. He was grateful for the assistance and the company. Some days were unbearable being alone in the jailhouse. Now he had someone to talk to, bounce ideas off of and aid in the capturing of any outlaws.

Bill figured Robby Fuller killed his wife, and Gabe agreed. But the doc had other notions. Pete was forward in his thoughts about Miss Montgomery and that Gabe needed to investigate her. Unfortunately, she was a suspect until the cause of death was found.

"I'm headed over to the doc's," he said to Bill.

The older man lounged in a chair in the corner with his feet propped on a small table. He tipped his hat up. "Cause of death will be from the beatin' the poor gal took."

"You're probably right, but I need to be sure."

Bill let his hat slip back down over his forehead to rest on his nose. Gabe exited the jailhouse, stepping out into the afternoon sunshine.

He'd yet to come across Robby to question him. He had a few choice words for the bastard too. A man did not lay his hands on a woman. Poor Mrs. Fuller had felt the abuse many times over according to Fern. The thought sickened him.

The school bell rang, and he watched as the children burst from the doors as if a wild fire were chasing them. Not much had changed since when he used to attend. He couldn't wait to escape the four walls—to be free of the lectures and math problems.

He entered the doctor's office. The strong scent of iodine filled his nostrils and burned. He ran the side of his hand under his nose to mask the scent and stop himself from sneezing. A small desk sat to his left, polished with neatly stacked papers. Two chairs served as a waiting area, and to the right of that was a closed door.

He knocked.

He heard shuffling inside before the door swung open. He stepped aside as the doctor escorted a young, very attractive, Angela Davenport through the office and to the front door.

"Sheriff," she said, her cheeks aglow.

"Ma'am."

"Have a lovely day, Miss Davenport," Pete said.

The girl nodded, smiling shyly before she left.

"What can I help you with, Sheriff?" he asked after the door closed.

He sensed a bit of irritation within the doctor, but ignored it and attended to other pressing matters, like who killed Sarah Fuller.

"Do you know the cause of Mrs. Fuller's death?"

"I do, and I can't say I'm surprised."

He followed the man through the examining room and into another small room where Mrs. Fuller lay naked on a long table. Pete yanked the blanket from a nearby chair and threw it across the woman's body haphazardly.

"Come here and look."

Gabe stepped closer to the corpse. He gazed down at Sarah Fuller's bruised and swollen face. The skin had begun to turn a light shade of blue, and the body appeared stiff.

"What exactly am I looking for?"

"Do you see it?"

Gabe had no idea what in hell the other man was talking about and answered with a growl.

Pete reached behind him to grab a magnify glass.

"Here, look through this."

Gabe took the piece, and Pete positioned it just above Mrs. Fuller's mouth.

"Do you see the faint white line along her lips?"

"Yes."

"Now, look to the left. What do you see?"

"White dots that look like salt or possibly sugar at the corner of her mouth?"

"Yes."

"What is it?"

"The line on her lips and the white residue are telling us what Mrs. Fuller ate before she passed."

"And what is that?"

Pete took the magnify glass from him and placed it on the table. "Sheriff, have you ever heard of the plant known as doll's eye?"

He shook his head.

"It is a very poisonous plant that does not grow around these parts."

Gabe knew where this conversation was going and he didn't like it.

"Mrs. Fuller ingested the plant. That is what killed her."

"How can you be sure? There are many plants that are used for good. Are you certain this doll's eye is fatal if ingested?"

"Quite. I have studied poisonous plants for some

time now. It is what has ended Sarah Fuller's life. When I looked into her throat there was bile on the lining of the esophagus. She also wet herself."

He raised a brow. He had no idea what any of this meant.

"Signs of the heart seizing or stopping caused by a reaction to the plant."

He ran his hand down the front of his face and sighed.

"If you do not believe me ask Miss Montgomery. She was the one who gave it to Mrs. Fuller."

"How can you be sure of that?"

"She grows the poisonous plant within her garden."

He ran his back teeth together. He didn't want Fern to be involved. Damn it.

"You will have to arrest her."

The man didn't need to tell him how to do his bloody job. He knew what needed to be done.

"Is there anything else?"

"You only have to ingest a small amount to kill you. Mrs. Fuller would not intentionally do herself in."

Gabe couldn't be so sure. A life with an abusive husband may have pushed her to do something drastic such as end her own life.

"You cannot think she'd kill herself?"

"It is a possibility."

Pete slammed his hand down onto the table. The utensils vibrated, offering a high-pitched clinking that pierced Gabe's ears.

He cringed. He'd always had sensitive hearing, ever since his older brother Hank blasted a shotgun next to his head when he was seven. He hadn't thought about his brother in some time, and the memory picked at a nerve. He rubbed the back of his neck to ease the tension.

"Do you know why Doctor Montgomery named his daughters after plants?"

"Can't say I do."

"Fern, Poppy and Ivy are all poisonous. Those girls have venom in their blood…just as their father did."

"You can't be serious. From what I've heard Doctor Montgomery was respected here in Manchester."

"You're not very bright, Sheriff. Fern Montgomery needs to be arrested. She is the one who gave the doll's eye to Mrs. Fuller."

"How do you know it was Fern who gave it to her?"

"As I stated earlier, she grows it in her garden."

He had said that, but Gabe was so shocked Fern could be involved he'd dismissed it.

The other man narrowed his eyes. The room reeked of his frustration. Gabe didn't care. It was his job to investigate all matters, and he wasn't so sure Fern gave Mrs. Fuller the poisonous plant.

"Do you fancy the herb collector, Sheriff?"

Gabe frowned.

"Have you taken a liking to her petite frame, thick mane of chestnut locks and tart mouth?"

Did the doctor have feelings for Fern? The other man was happily married to Lucy, the schoolmarm. Talk around town was they were trying for a baby and everyone anticipated the good news.

"My feelings are none of your damn business, Doc. I am doing my job and looking at all aspects of this situation."

"I hope so, Sheriff. I'd hate to see you lose your job over bad judgment and lack of skills."

Gabe leaned forward. It took all his strength not to wrap his hands around Pete's wormy neck and squeeze.

"I don't take kindly to threats," he growled.

"Then I suggest you do your job."

"It's best if you stay away from Miss Montgomery until I've finished this investigation. I better not hear of you sending Robby Fuller her way again."

"You cannot tell me what to do, Sheriff. I am a law abiding citizen of this town that, may I remind you, sits on the town council."

He reached across the corpse, grabbing the other man by the collar of his shirt and pulling him across the table.

"I'll not warn you again. The next time you threaten me, I'll make damn sure you're the one laying on this table."

Pete's Adam's apple bobbed up and down, and eyes big and round, he nodded.

"Leave Mrs. Fuller as she is. I will be back this afternoon with Miss Montgomery."

The other man nodded when Gabe realized he still held him by the collar. He released him and watched as the lengthy man fixed his shirt.

He tipped his hat and walked out of the room just as Lucy Miller was coming in.

"Ma'am."

"Sheriff, what a pleasant surprise." Her voice was faint and breathy. He'd wondered how she was able to control the children without a stern demeanor and commanding vocals.

"How was your day, sweetheart?" Pete went to his wife with open arms. She flew into them, her face flushed with love and affection.

"Wonderful, Pete," she answered into his neck. "Were you able to find out how Sarah died?"

"Yes, it was as I figured."

"I just can't see Fern being responsible," Lucy said.

"It is as I've said all along, dear, the Montgomery girls are poison, and now they've killed one of Manchester's own." He squeezed Lucy to him. "I can't abide her ways any longer. People's lives depend on my intuition."

Gabe had to fight to keep from throwing up; the tone in the other man's voice was enough to make him sick. He tipped his hat to both of them, and walked out into the sunlight.

"Good day, Sheriff." Mayor Smith leaned against the brick building.

He'd been waiting for him no doubt. Gabe was starting to see how Fern must feel being bullied by the two most powerful men in town.

"Mayor."

"I hear Fern is responsible for Mrs. Fuller's death. Can't say I'm surprised."

"News travels fast around here."

Aggravated at the robust man and his assumptions, he kept walking.

"I assume you're going to arrest Miss Montgomery."

He stopped to stare at the man. His jaw flexed as he rubbed his molars together.

"Since there is no room in the jail for her, she can await the judge at my place. I'll keep an eye on her."

He bet the bastard would. Gabe didn't like any of this. The more he got to know the doctor and mayor he was beginning to see things differently.

"*If* I arrest Miss Montgomery, she will stay in my care and no one else's," he growled.

"A woman can't go around figuring she has all of these rights. Fern is a hazard to the wellbeing of those in Manchester."

He flexed his fists and picked up his pace, leaving the mayor behind.

"I hope you'll be paying Fern Montgomery a visit today," Smith called after him. "And my offer still stands."

Chapter Five

Fern placed three plates on the table. One fried egg, a sliced tomato and a piece of bread on each. A small meal that would have Poppy complaining she was sure, but it was all they had. Most of her patrons couldn't afford to pay for the advice and herbs she gave them. Instead, they offered food, milk, or fabric and some nothing at all. She understood how they couldn't give money, what with some of their husbands not aware they visited. She wished more people of Manchester were as open-minded as the women and few men who came to see her.

The plants had aided those in need for centuries. It was not some newfangled thing, as Doctor Miller seemed insistent upon portraying. He acted as if she were selling potions and fake remedies. The greenery, flowers, roots and vegetables did the healing on their own. Her customers were proof of that.

However all of it didn't hide the fact there was no money. She was desperate for supplies. The barn needed repair, the cabin could use some care, and the lack of meat, eggs and milk were starting to wear on even her.

She sighed and placed her hands upon her hips.

"It will have to do for now," she whispered.

"No, it will not," Poppy growled from the doorway.

Fern rolled her eyes.

"I am starved, wasting away to nothin', and you offer me this for breakfast?"

"It is all we have."

"Last night you sent me to bed with little more than greens from the garden. I nearly died of hunger. And now I've awoken famished to this?" she shrieked.

Always drama. Poppy was known for it, and today Fern wasn't in the mood.

"Quiet down and eat your damn breakfast," she snapped.

"Why won't you let me go hunt for a rabbit or a deer?"

"Unless it is on our land…the answer is no."

"I am good with the shotgun. Why don't you trust me?

"It isn't a matter of trust, Poppy. It is about safety, and you're a sixteen-year-old girl out in the forest all by yourself. What if something happened?"

"Bah! I am capable of protecting myself and this family."

She couldn't argue that, but Fern worried she'd come across a band of Indians or outlaws, and she'd never see her sister again.

"Anything but more greens and bread," the girl moaned.

"We've discussed this. If you cannot find prey within the vicinity of our land we will eat what God has provided to us."

"But, there hasn't been anything in my traps for days. If you don't let me venture soon we will starve!"

"Quit being so dramatic. We will be fine."

"I love tomatoes," Ivy chirped from the hallway, her golden hair tousled and the signs of sleep still in her eyes.

Fern smiled. The girl was genuine and sweet, not like their sister.

"How is your head?"

Ivy's blue eyes smiled. "Good as gold."

"Wonderful. That means the peppermint tea worked."

Ivy had been suffering with awful headaches for the last month. Fern had been searching for something to ease the pain and take them away completely. The young girl had been quiet and withdrawn the past few weeks. Fern didn't understand why. She'd sat with her a few times, trying to get her to open up, but nothing ever came of the conversations. There was something Ivy wasn't telling her, but with other problems arising, she couldn't dwell on the situation and prayed that things would work themselves out.

Poppy sat down at the table, brows furrowed, and dug into her breakfast. The girl was born sulking. Fern shook her head and took a chair beside Ivy. The sun shone through the window to chase the last of the cool air out of the cabin. The afternoon would bring warmer temperatures typical for a July day, and she'd welcome them while toiling in the garden.

Poppy jumped up and went for the shotgun by the door.

"What are you doing?"

"We've got company and it ain't welcome," the girl replied as she checked to make sure the weapon was loaded.

Fern peered out the window, and her stomach dropped. Robby Fuller sat on top of his horse. His unshaven face shadowed with brown whiskers. Bloodshot eyes framed with dark circles. He had a pasty sheen to his skin that showed a night of mourning followed by the bottle and likely more than one.

She leaned down and whispered into Ivy's ear, "Stay inside. No matter what."

The girl nodded.

She reached for their father's Colt .45 and opened the door.

"You!" Robby lifted his gun and pointed it at Fern.

"I'd put that gun down if I were you," Poppy said, coming out from behind Fern. She stepped a few feet to the side, cocked the shotgun and trained it on Robby.

He fixed his gaze on the girl but did not falter his aim on Fern.

"I ain't scared of a little girl."

Poppy shrugged. "We're all the same age when we shoot a gun."

"Ha! You ain't nothin', with or without that barrel."

"We shall see when you're full of led, twitchin' and bleedin' like a gutted pig."

"You're a sass mouthed bitch ain't ya?" he said and then spat onto the ground.

"And you're a sissy bastard hittin' Sarah the way you did."

Fern's heart stopped.

Robby's cheeks flamed red, his bottom lip curled as his eyes emitted revulsion. She glanced at Poppy holding the shotgun ready to fire, and back to Robby, his face distorted and angled.

"Don't you talk about my Sarah," he yelled. "She was precious."

"Well you got a funny way of showin' it, layin' your fists on her the way ya did," Poppy said.

Robby bit down on his lower lip and groaned followed by a loud screech. "You're both gonna die today." He pulled another gun from his belt and aimed it at Poppy.

"You're as dumb as a castrated bull," the girl spat.

He gaped at her.

"You have two guns aimed on ya, and this one is gonna blast a hole the size of Texas through you. You haven't a chance."

"Shut the hell up, bitch."

"Poppy," Fern warned.

"You may shoot one of us, but I'll make damned

sure there ain't nothin' left of your middle but a gaping hole."

Robby growled, and to Fern's surprise he holstered his guns, swung his horse around and rode away. She turned to leave when out of the corner of her eye she saw him stop.

He twisted in the saddle, pointed his gun at Poppy, and fired.

"No!" Fern shouted.

The sound of the shot bounced off the mountains around them. Robby dug his heels into his horse's side and the animal cantered away, disappearing through the bush. Her throat tight and dry she swallowed the dusty air. Poppy lay on the ground unmoving a few feet from her, a crumpled heap on the porch.

She leapt toward her sister. *Not Poppy. Please.* Fern placed her fingers to Poppy's neck and felt a pulse. *Thank goodness.* She spotted the blood on the boards and rolled Poppy over so she could get a better look. There was no telling how injured she was. If the bullet struck an organ she could bleed out in seconds.

Poppy's left side was wet with blood, and Fern ripped the seam on her shirt to get a better look. She pushed away the girl's stay, and exhaled followed by a pitiful cry. The bullet had grazed her sister's side, leaving a gap in the skin that would need to be stitched. No organs were damaged, and she'd not be digging out a bullet today, thank the Saints.

She scanned the porch behind Poppy and the cabin wall for the bullet. A flash of silver glinted in the back of the bench their father had made for their mother when they lived in Boston. Built from pine, he ordered the carpenter to make the bench sturdy and strong—to last a lifetime. Unfortunately, their lifetime together was cut short. The thick pine had stopped the bullet from going into the cabin and possibly striking Ivy.

Thank you, Pa.

Poppy stirred and Fern once again placed her attention on her injured sister.

"Poppy? Poppy, you need to get up so we can get you inside."

The girl shot up and reached for her gun.

"It's okay. We are okay."

"Where is that son of a bitch?" She winced, the pain in her side causing her grief.

"Gone."

She wiggled, trying to sit up.

"Slow movements, you were shot."

Poppy's blue eyes grew round. "I was?"

Fern nodded.

"Am I dyin'?"

"No, but I need to get you inside and cleaned up. Your side is open; the bullet caught your skin."

"Holy shit."

"Poppy."

"Bloody hell."

Fern glared at her.

"Well, let's get to it then. My side is achin' like hell."

Fern called for Ivy and the girl rushed out, fear present on her youthful face.

"Is Poppy okay?"

"Yes, we are all safe. I need your help getting her inside."

"Is she shot?"

"Of course I was shot, tart. You think I'd be laying here like I am if I wasn't?" Poppy grumbled.

Together they were able to get Poppy inside and onto her bed.

"I'll need you to boil some water, and grab the yarrow leaves from the shelf, please."

The girl hurried to do as she was told.

Fern removed Poppy's shirt and denims. She instructed her to press the ripped pieces of cotton to the wound while she searched for her sewing kit and whiskey to disinfect the needle and thread.

She placed her palms onto the counter, bent her head and said a silent prayer that Robby Fuller didn't come back while she tended to her sister. She'd have no choice but to protect them and that meant the possibility of killing him. She wasn't sure she could end someone's life. Right or wrong, good or evil, she doubted she'd be able to pull the trigger. Her stomach flipped. She rubbed her palms together to dry the moisture from them and shuddered.

She blew the dark strand of hair from her face only to have it come back to the exact same spot. Tucking the errant hair behind her ear, she peeked out the window. If Robby lurked outside Fern would need to defend them whether she liked it or not. She glanced at the shotgun propped up beside the door. With Poppy injured she'd need to take on the girl's shooting skills and the thought was unsettling.

Fern pulled the bandage snug against Poppy's side. The girl was out thanks to the strong chamomile tea she'd made. Her sister was tough, but she wasn't so sure the girl could handle the ten stitches Fern had sewn into her side.

She sat back and assessed her work. It would do and keep infection from setting in. She'd need to check on the wound every few hours, maybe apply some more yarrow if the skin looked red and puffy. She glanced at the jar on the small table beside the bed. Green yarrow leaves lay inside. She'd placed them directly onto the wound. If that didn't work she had a jar of ground yarrow as well.

Chapter Six

Fern exited the garden room off of the kitchen and closed the door behind her. She'd retreated to the tiny room after mending Poppy, not comfortable with going outside and plucking away at the garden there. She enjoyed inspecting the garlic, thyme, rosemary, lavender and mint she grew within the wooden walls. The job calmed her nerves and after this morning she needed it.

She looked at Poppy still asleep beneath the heavy quilt and wondered when she'd wake. It'd been hours since she'd stirred, and the beet soup simmering on the stove was ready to eat. Poppy wouldn't be pleased with the vegetable soup, but it would assist in making her feel better. Reluctant to wake her, Fern went and sat beside Ivy, who was practicing her numbers at the table.

"How are things going?" she asked.

Ivy blew out a loud breath.

"Still struggling?"

"Yes."

She placed her hand over the girl's and squeezed.

"The practice will help. Soon you'll be able to solve all those problems without writing things down first."

A soft knock on the door stole her attention from Ivy. She glanced at the Colt lying above the door. *Robby.* Heart hammering against her ribcage, she fingered the curtain, pulling it back an inch to peek through. Blue calico was all she needed to see to know they weren't in any danger. She released the breath she'd been holding and hurried to the door.

A wide brimmed sunbonnet shaded May Hansen's flawless skin and sable eyes.

"Good afternoon, May."

"Hello, Fern," she said. Her voice, unusually deep for a woman, held a hint of pleasure and temptation to it. She'd often wondered if the woman had been ridiculed when she was young because of it. Widowed two years ago, May had been left with three children to care for.

"Please, come in." She stepped aside to allow her to pass.

Fern didn't need to say anything to Ivy; the young girl quickly cleaned up her mess at the table and went to sit with Poppy, who was still asleep.

She pulled out a chair and motioned for May to take a seat, before sitting across from her. She smiled at the other woman, but sensed something was off. May was usually demure, quiet even, but was always friendly. Today she held herself at a distance, her shoulders rigid and mouth straight.

"What can I help you with?"

May removed her white gloves and placed them on the table in front of her before meeting Ferns eyes.

"I'm in need of some…something to help with my cycle."

She smiled.

"Sure. What exactly is the problem?"

"I…I have not bled."

"It is common for the cycle to be delayed due to lack of sleep, over exertion or worry."

"No, it is not that. I've been without it for three weeks."

"You have not expelled at all this month?"

She shook her head.

"What is your age, May?"

"I am thirty-three this August."

She was bewildered at how the widow could not be menstruating, and yet be far too young for her body to start the cycle of menses.

"Have you fallen, or injured yourself in any way?"

"I am not ill, Fern. I am…" May leaned in. "I am with child."

"How is that possible?" Fern couldn't help her reply and slapped her hand over her mouth. "My apologies," she mumbled.

"It is okay. I do not wish to discuss the how or why of this incident, but instead the ending of this pregnancy."

Ferns throat grew thick. She loved helping people with her plants, but these requests were most difficult for her to do. Her stomach turned.

"Are you sure?" she asked, placing her hand on May's.

The corner of her mouth lifted in a small smile. "I am not sure of anything."

"Let me put on some tea and we can talk."

"No, I…I left the children at home and cannot stay." She raised pleading eyes toward her. "I don't want to do this, but you need to understand I cannot have a child out of wedlock. I will be an outcast. The town will shun me. I cannot place that kind of ridicule upon my children."

"I understand your concern. Is it possible for your gentleman friend to make an honest woman out of you?"

"It cannot happen."

"Surely he will offer for you once he knows of the child."

"He was the one who sent me here."

That changed everything. Fern understood May's desperation. She may not agree with her decision, but she'd help her…it was what she did.

"Let me see what I have in the garden room." She left to go search out the parsley she grew for flavor in their foods, ailments, and to bring on a missed or late cycle. The green leafed herb would cause the cervix to contract thus forcing the body into its regular rotation.

She grabbed her scissors off of the makeshift counter and snipped a few leaves from the plant. She wrapped them in brown paper and brought them to May.

"Boil water to make tea. Place all of the leaves into the cup of steaming water and let steep. Once they've been steeped sip the contents until it is all gone. By morning you will bleed."

May took the contents from her and held them to her breast. Tears shone in her red-brown eyes and she stood.

"Thank you, Fern."

She placed an arm around the other woman's shoulders and walked her to the door.

"I am here if you ever need anything."

"Please…if I could ask you to keep this between us?"

"Of course. I adhere to a strict privacy rule when it comes to those I see."

"Thank you."

She smiled.

May opened the door to leave, but before exiting she turned toward Fern. "I almost forgot to mention it. On my travels here, I saw Robby Fuller watching your place from on top of Blue Hill. I'm assuming he's heard of poor Sarah and blames you."

"Your assumption is correct." She glanced back at Poppy. "He's already paid us a visit."

May's eyes expanded when she noticed Poppy sleeping in the far corner of the room.

"Oh my, what happened?"

"He shot Poppy this morning. The bullet tore into her skin good, but did not lodge itself inside and it was a clean tear, thank the Saints."

"Will she be all right?"

"She will as long as infection doesn't set in."

May nodded and gave Poppy one more look before leaving to head home.

Fern closed the door and leaned against it, her forehead resting gently on the wood. Robby was waiting up on Blue Hill for a reason, and Fern had an awful feeling it was for nightfall. It was easier to sneak up on someone in the dark. She'd have a hard time seeing him until he was right at their door. She swallowed past the fear that grew thick in her throat. She'd need to remain on watch all night to make sure that didn't happen.

A loud knock shook the door and vibrated against her forehead. She jumped back, lungs cold with panic. With a trembling hand she reached for the pistol above the door.

The gun felt foreign in her grip, and she dropped her arm to her side unsure of what to do with it. She motioned for Ivy to climb up the ladder to her room. Once the girl had disappeared, she faced the door once more. She slid one booted foot forward when another knock startled her and the pistol almost slipped from her fingers. The weight of the gun pulled her shoulder down, and she shifted her weight to her left leg.

"Who's there?" she called.

"Sheriff Bennett."

She relaxed her stance, but not yet comfortable placing the gun onto the table she clutched it tight within her trembling hand. The brass door handle seemed heavier than usual as she turned it. Instead of waiting for her to open the door, he pressed a thick arm across it and the wooden door swung open. Sheriff Bennett's wide shoulders filled the entrance and blocked the afternoon sun shining bright behind him.

She stumbled backward; the gun slipped from her hand and fell onto the floor. The impact with the hardwood floor caused the Colt to discharge. The bullet whizzed between Sheriff Bennett's legs, landing somewhere outside.

His eyes grew big before turning downward into a frightening glare. He advanced on her, his broad chest heaving. She tried to run, but her legs wouldn't obey. Instead, they planted themselves to the floor. He was coming closer. There was nothing left to do, but squeeze her eyes shut and wait for the blow. She felt his breath upon her face, and the cold as her blood froze with fear.

When he didn't strike her, she opened her eyes.

He picked up the gun, placed it on the table and turned toward her.

"You should learn how to use that," he said, his voice calm.

She was sure he'd do her harm. The anger upon his face told her so. But as she stared at him, and then examined herself, he'd not laid one finger upon her. Admiration pressed on her heart, filling her eyes with tears. *He was the enemy, just like all the others.* She blinked, disguising the emotion she suddenly felt for him and walked toward the table. She picked up the Colt and placed it on the ledge above the door.

When she could trust her voice to speak without quivering, she said, "I can shoot just fine."

"Yeah, I can see that."

"Why are you here?"

He sighed, crossed his arms, unfolded them and crossed them again.

He was nervous and that meant one thing. She inhaled slowly trying to ease the twisting in her stomach…he'd come for her.

"Can we sit down?"

She motioned to the table and chairs a few feet away.

"I just came from Doc's."

She waited.

"He was able to find out how Mrs. Fuller died."

"You came here to tell me what I already know?

That her husband killed her?" Frustration clawed at her voice and it sounded pitted.

"It wasn't her husband, Fern."

"Well then who was it?"

"Doc seems to think it was you."

"Of course he does. Mayor Smith too I suppose?"

He nodded.

"I didn't do it. She was my friend."

"I have to ask you some questions, and I'll need your honesty in answering them."

"I've not lied to you thus far, Sheriff, and I won't start now."

"Please, call me Gabe."

She wasn't comfortable with calling him anything. He was here to put Sarah's murder on her. Robby Fuller killed his wife and it was quite obvious she'd need to prove it.

"Do you grow doll's eye within your garden?"

"No. It is grown in two pots in my garden room." She pointed to the room behind him.

"Why do you grow it in there?"

"Because it is not from around here and would die if planted outside."

"Is it poisonous?"

"Yes."

"Why do you have it then?"

"My father brought it from Boston. Although toxic, the plant in small doses can aid in childbirth, menstruation, headaches, colds and coughs. I've only used it a few times for birthing. At the time it was the only remedy that worked."

"How can a plant so poisonous be used for those things?"

"It is how you prepare it, such as with all of my herbs, plants and vegetables."

"I don't understand."

"The doll's eye has berries, leaves, a stem and roots all of which are toxic. I harvest the root for use in a tea. I take small amounts and place them into boiling water. Once steeped I remove the root and allow my patient to drink the liquid, thus relieving them of their discomfort while of course not poisoning them."

"You do not give them the berries directly?"

"Heavens no. That would kill them within an hour. The berries are the most potent part of the plant."

"How do you know this?"

She repositioned herself in the chair, and pulled her eyes from his scrutinizing gaze. She'd seen what the berries could do, and she'd not tell anyone of it either.

"Fern, how do you know the berries are the most poisonous part of the plant?"

"I just know."

"That is not a good enough answer."

"It will have to do."

"It doesn't, and unless you want to spend your days in jail, I suggest you answer me."

"Jail? You'd lock me up without any evidence, without any cause?"

"I have plenty of evidence that suggests you killed Sarah."

She bristled. "Such as?"

"You're the only one within a hundred miles who grows doll's eye which is what Mrs. Fuller was poisoned with. You admitted to giving it to patients, and Sarah's last known place before she died was here."

"I did not give Sarah the plant," she growled. "You forget my father was a doctor, who was advanced in the healing remedies of what the earth grows. He taught me." She wasn't lying. Pa had taught her, but she didn't divulge more.

"I see. It still doesn't explain how Mrs. Fuller got the doll's eye and why she ate it."

She tapped her fingers on the table, trying to keep her composure when all she wanted to do was lunge at him. How could he think she'd kill anyone, especially her friend? She was not a murderer. She wouldn't harm a soul. She wanted to help those in need, offer a different way of getting well instead of opium, morphine, amputation and infected wounds.

That she was not welcome in Manchester was evident, but to accuse her of killing Sarah was absurd. Acceptance by the townsmen was not going to happen, she could see that now, but she wasn't about to give up. It was her calling to work with the herbs and plants. Like her father, she felt pride at being able to help those in need, and she wouldn't let Sheriff Bennett, Doc Miller, Mayor Smith or anyone take that from her.

"How did you know I grew doll's eye here?" she asked. She hadn't told anyone she grew it and in fact when using it on Penny Williams last year, she'd not said what it was.

"Doctor Miller stated it this morning while I was in his examining room."

"Did he say how he knew I grew the plant here?"

"I didn't ask him."

"Maybe you should."

"He hasn't come out here?"

"Yes, a few times, but never within my home and

definitely not inside my garden room where it is grown."

"What has he come for?"

"To accuse me of using fake elixirs, and to scare me into leaving Manchester mostly."

"He hasn't searched the garden or inspected the grounds?"

"As I've told you it wouldn't matter if he did. The plant is grown in the garden room not outside."

"This doesn't bode well for you, Fern."

She could see that, but she'd stand her ground. "I did not give the doll's eye to Sarah."

"Has anyone been in your garden room?"

"Yes, of course. On occasion I've brought my patrons in with me to show them some of the plants."

"Have you shown the doll's eye to anyone?"

She shook her head. "Even if they saw it, they wouldn't know what it was. The plant doesn't grow here."

"And Pete Miller has not been in your home?"

"Never."

He eyed her.

"This is my land, and just because I am a woman, does not mean I am weak."

"Never said that, but I do see how three young females can be taken advantage of."

"Not with Poppy wielding a gun at them."

At the mention of her name, the girl moaned, and Fern left him at the table to tend to her.

Chapter Seven

Gabe hadn't noticed Poppy asleep on the cot in the corner of the room. He followed Fern to where her sister lay. He watched as she pulled back the blanket covering the girl and carefully removed the fabric wrapped around her middle.

At first he'd assumed she was sick, but when Fern began unraveling the linen from Poppy's side, he'd known it was much worse.

"What happened to her?"

Fern ignored him while she let the fabric fall into a pile on the floor. A large gash, stitched and sparsely covered in blood soaked leaves stared up at him. He glanced at Poppy's ashen face and knew infection had set in.

"When did this happen?"

"This morning." She placed her palm to Poppy's forehead.

"Does she have a fever?"

She nodded, and her blue eyes crinkled with worry.

"I don't understand this. I cleaned the wound, disinfected the needle and thread. I even placed yarrow leaves across the gash to protect it from infection."

She pulled the damp leaves from Poppy's side and placed them onto the table beside the bed. The skin around the stitching was swollen and red.

"How did she get the wound?"

"Robby Fuller shot her this morning." She said the words so calmly he wondered if he'd heard her right. He'd been here for a half hour and she hadn't uttered a damn word about the incident this morning.

"When were you going to divulge that bit of information to me?" he growled.

"I didn't see the point." She glanced back at him. "You were too busy accusing me of murder."

"Damn it, I was doing my job." He was still stunned she hadn't said a word about the shooting. Why would she hide that from him? Didn't she trust him? He stared at her, back rigid, shoulders straight and head tilted away from him. Her guard was up, and he was the reason. Trust didn't come easy for someone like Fern, and with most of the town against her it wasn't likely she'd be giving that sentiment away anytime soon.

It explained why she almost shot him when he arrived. He guessed she couldn't use the gun any better than a schoolmarm. Poppy was a crack shot. Now that she was injured with what looked to be a nasty infection, Fern was left to defend the family and their land.

"Did you dig the bullet out?"

I didn't have to. It grazed her skin, leaving the long tear."

"Did he only fire one shot?"

"Yes, and took off into the hills."

"You hadn't the time to fire back?"

She paused. Her hands shook, and he noted the tremble in her voice. "I didn't."

"Why the hell not?"

"I…I was worried about Poppy," she snapped.

"How did you know he wasn't aiming at you? Natural instinct is to defend oneself. Why didn't you?"

"I don't know."

He'd bet there was more to her denial than what she was saying. In fact he'd trade his horse if he were wrong. Fern Montgomery wouldn't hurt a fly even if the damn thing were hell bent on killing her—which meant she didn't poison her friend on purpose...but possibly by accident.

She could feel his gaze upon her and remained the same, trying to ignore him. He asked such personal questions, ones she was not prepared to answer. She straightened. Right now he was the least of her worries. Poppy was ill, and she needed to make her better.

She stared at the blazing wound. It didn't make sense. How had Poppy gotten an infection? She'd only been shot this morning, and Fern had cleaned the lesion right away. She needed to think—to go through the list of healing herbs in her mind and find one that would work. It didn't help that Gabe was standing so close, blocking her concentration.

"Fern?" Ivy's feathery voice floated toward her.

She glanced up at her sister, cheeks flushed, blonde hair hanging loose from her braids to frame round cheeks. She loved both of her sisters very much, and the thought of something happening to them caused her insides to ache and her throat to close.

"Yes?"

"Is Poppy all right?"

She didn't believe in lying. The truth should always be told.

"She has an infection, but I am going to do everything I can to get her better."

"Is she sick like mama was?"

She tipped her head away from Gabe so he wouldn't see the tears in her eyes. Their mother died in Boston when Ivy was five. The death traumatized the whole family, Fern especially.

"No, my sweet. It is not the same as mama."

The girl nodded, came toward her, and laid her head on Fern's shoulder.

"You'll make Poppy well. I know it."

She smiled and squeezed her sister to her in a long hug.

"Let's get to it, shall we?"

Ivy nodded.

Fern slapped her hands together. She needed to find a new remedy for the infection. Staying busy was best so she didn't go insane with worry. She took the soiled bandages and handed them to Ivy.

"Place these in the bucket outside the door. We will burn them later."

"Yes, Ma'am."

"What can I do?" Gabe asked.

She'd forgotten he was still there.

"You mean to stay?"

His dark eyes softened.

"If it's okay."

She didn't know what to say, how to answer him. No one had offered help to her before, even when pa was sick. She wasn't sure what to make of Gabe. Could she trust him, and if she did, what would he do when he found out about her past?

"I will need water brought in from the well and boiled on the stove."

He nodded and left to do her bidding.

Fern hurried into the garden room. She searched the shelves of plants and herbs. She reached for the aloe on the third shelf and placed it behind her on the small table; she'd need it once the infection was gone. The sticky salve from the prickly leaves was great for diminishing redness and irritation once the wound had scabbed. She thumbed the thyme, rosemary and basil then she came to the slippery elm. A green leafed plant used for burns, skin infections, swelling of the lungs and throat due to sickness. This is what she'd use. She'd need to make a powder substance in order for the plant to work quickly on Poppy's wound.

With the pot of slippery elm held tight to her

bosom, she went to the kitchen to prepare the plant to be ground.

Gabe had put the water on to boil and was watching her intently.

"What are you doing?"

"I am going to use this to make a poultice and draw out the infection."

She placed the leaves in the stone mortar, and using the pestle, she ground them into a grainy powder.

"What kind of plant is that?"

"Slippery elm. It is used by most Indian tribes to heal burns, skin infections and when steeped, it cures the throat of swelling and pain."

"How do you know all of this?"

"My father taught me, and I read…a lot."

"Read what?"

"My father had acquired *Culpeper's Complete Herbal* book written by Nicolas Culpeper in 1653. He paid a fair price for it too. He was passionate about studying the text and applying it to his practice."

She stood on tiptoes and grabbed the jar of beeswax beside the homemade blueberry jam.

"What is that?"

She couldn't tell if he was curious or if he was still investigating her, and she hadn't the time to distinguish between the two.

"This is beeswax. It is good for inflammation and swelling. I will place the poultice on the wound then lather a thin layer of beeswax to seal it."

"You have bees here too?"

She scooped up the mortar, cradling it within the crook of her arm. Before she could grab the beeswax, he placed his large hand over the lid and lifted it from the counter.

"No, I buy the wax and honey from Mr. Davenport. He lives a few miles east of here."

"I know where the Davenports live."

She peeked at him through her lashes. The furrow of his brows told her he was not happy with her cheeky comment. She shrugged off his irritation. Pleasing him was the last thing on her mind.

"I'll need the water, please."

He placed the beeswax on the table beside Poppy's bed and fetched the water.

She leaned back to allow him to place the pot onto the floor in front of her. His nearness caused her heart to race and cheeks to flush. She held her breath until he was standing beside her again, and she reached for the cloth. Careful not to burn herself, she dipped the cloth into the scalding water before she gently wiped the festering wound.

"He doesn't think you're crazy like the other men in town?"

"Who?"

"Mr. Davenport."

"He does, but he needs to make a living as well."

"I see."

She paused, annoyed at his brash conclusions of her. He knew nothing about her or her sisters, yet he was no different than all the others who cast their judgment on them.

"Do you?"

"Yes, I understand why men won't come to see you."

"Is that so, Sheriff."

"You're a woman."

"By golly you've got it. All of this time I thought it was because they were sissies."

"Very funny. I mean to say the men of Manchester feel threatened by you. It is clear you know what you're doing."

"Why, thank you, but I think it is much simpler than that."

"How so?"

"I am a woman, yes, but they see all women as married, mothers and serving their men."

"You don't see yourself as a wife or mother?"

She snickered.

"I am too strong willed and independent for any man to look my way."

He stepped toward her, and placed his hand upon her shoulder. She leaned away from him until he no longer touched her. She did not need his remorse. She chose this life and she'd live it, even if that meant alone.

Chapter Eight

Gabe searched the bench on the front porch where Fern had said the bullet was lodged. He was sure the slug had come apart and that was why Poppy had caught the infection so soon. He needed to be certain before he told Fern she'd have to open the girl up and dig out the remaining bullet fragments.

Thankfully the shot hadn't struck an organ; the result could've been fatal. As it was now, Fern was working overtime to keep the girl's fever and infection at bay.

He pulled the knife from the sheath on his belt when he spotted the metal slug in the backing of the pine bench. Careful not to wreck the family heirloom, he gently picked away at the bullet until it popped from the wood and into his hand.

It was as he expected, a piece of the bullet was missing. He clenched the shot within his fist. Was Robby Fuller's intention to kill Poppy Montgomery, or injure her? Gabe wasn't sure, but it did seem odd that Robby hadn't aimed at Fern instead. She was the one who befriended his wife, and who the doc accused of murder.

None of it made sense. He had a bad feeling Poppy wasn't the intended target. Someone else was behind Robby and his gun.

He rubbed the broken bullet between his finger and thumb. Small flakes of debris stuck to his skin. He glanced back at the cabin and then to the bullet. Poppy could have more than the one piece inside of her. It was no wonder the girl was burning up with infection. He rushed inside where Fern was applying a cool cloth to Poppy's forehead.

"How is she?" he asked, knowing the answer by the worried look on Fern's face.

"She is getting worse." Her blue eyes were shrouded in agony, begging him for an answer. "I don't know what else to do."

"I believe there is still some of the bullet left inside of her."

"What do you mean?"

He showed her the bullet.

She ran her hand across her forehead and down her face.

"I will need to reopen her."

He nodded.

"She is so sick already."

"It's the only way. Once you remove that bullet, you can start your healing prospects all over again. Right now, they're not doing anything."

"But she…she is very ill and I'll need…" she stammered.

"You can't fight the infection from the outside without removing that bullet."

"I know. She will need more than my herbs. She needs to fight it from the inside too."

"How does she do that?"

She chewed on her bottom lip.

He sensed her confusion and doubt. In the short time he'd known her she'd never let a hint of uncertainty escape past her lips.

"What do you need me to do?"

She lifted fearful eyes to his. "Get the doctor. He'll know of something else to give her, better than what I have here."

"Are you sure?"

"I…I'm…"

"Fern?"

"I think that'd be best."

He stared down at her, seated on the short stool beside her sister, hair messed and tangled, eyes red with unshed tears, her bottom lip tucked between her teeth. He admired her. She'd cast her pride to the dogs to save her sister.

He placed his hand on her shoulder. His intention to comfort her, but when he touched her, his chest swelled and an ache he'd not known before resonated inside of him. Instead of yanking his hand away he left it there, and watched as she leaned toward him. She had no idea of the slight move she'd made, too caught up in her concern for Poppy, but he was fully aware of her—and the way she made him feel.

Fern paced the floor, stopping every few feet to peer outside for Gabe. He'd been gone for over two hours, and she was growing restless. Dusk had fallen, casting the yard in dark shadows. Poppy's condition had worsened in the time passed. She was now convulsing from the high fever. Fern needed to remove the stitches, but could not do it without Gabe and Doc Miller's help. She ordered Ivy to fetch more cool water from the well and went back to sit with her sister as another fit came over her.

Ivy came through the door, and she rushed to grab the bucket of water from her.

"I need you stay by the window and watch for Gabe." She saw the red circles around Ivy's eyes and knew the young girl had been crying while outside. She yearned to comfort her, but there was no time. Right now they needed to stay strong for Poppy.

"Things will work out," she whispered.

"Do you promise?" Ivy's bottom lip shook.

Fern couldn't answer her. How was she to promise something she had no control of? She was supposed to be able to help those in need with her plants, but she'd tried the two she used often and neither worked. Poppy's condition was her fault. She hadn't looked for any bullet fragments when cleaning the wound. If she'd done so her sister wouldn't be battling an infection that could kill her. She knew better. She assumed the bullet had made a clean break of the skin. She'd been wrong—very wrong. As all possibilities came to a head, she was finding it difficult to breathe.

"Fern?"

She met Ivy's eyes.

"Do you promise?"

"I—

The door opened, slamming against the kitchen

table. Gabe pushed a very disgruntled Pete Miller into the cabin.

"Sorry it took me so long. I had some negotiating to do," Gabe said as he glared at Pete.

"Yes, well now that you've dragged me here what is it you want me to do for the girl?" he yapped.

Fern steadied herself and took four deep breaths before answering the arrogant man.

"As you can see my sister is ill. I didn't think…" She wrung her hands. "I hadn't checked for any fragments of the bullet inside of her and instead I sewed her up. I've tried everything to heal the wound from the outside, but I'm afraid there is still some of the bullet to be removed."

"I am not surprised coming from a woman who does not have a medical degree. Do you see why operating your little garden of fixes is dangerous to the people of Manchester?"

"I see nothing of the sort. I am not blind to the fact that not all things can be cured with herbs, roots and plants. However, I do see the need for other remedies to the opium you seem to hand out like candy sticks."

"I can see I am not needed here." Pete turned to leave, but was stopped by Gabe's hand.

"You're staying." He turned his attention to Fern.

"What do you want us to do?"

"I think the best thing is to remove the stitches, find the missing piece, clean the wound and apply another poultice," she answered, feeling stronger with him there. "If Doctor Miller would give her something to kill the infection from the inside that would help."

"Do not tell me how to do my job, or what to give to your sister. I will check her over before I determine what she needs."

Fern stepped aside to allow him to come near Poppy.

"I should let her die. That will teach you to stop with all of this nonsense." He waved his hand in the air.

Gabe stepped toward him, and Fern grabbed his shirt.

"We need to help Poppy," she whispered.

"She is toxic," Pete said.

"We know that, Doc," Gabe growled. "It's from the bullet."

"I see. So you did not dig the bullet out?"

"No, it just grazed the skin, but a piece is still inside of her," Fern answered.

"Pathetic. You are a waste of good flesh and bones."

Fern inhaled but remained silent.

"Pete," Gabe snarled.

"I will need to open her up and dig for the missing piece."

"I will help," Fern answered.

"No, you will not. In fact you will wait outside while I operate."

Her stomach twisted, and the hairs on the back of her neck stood. "I will remain here beside you."

He looked at Gabe. "Remove her at once."

"No can do, Doc. This is her place, and that is her sister."

The man blew out a loud breath and rummaged through his bag. "Stay out of my way," he ground out.

Fern stepped to the end of the bed as he cut the stitches and pulled them from Poppy's inflamed skin. The gash oozed a dark red with strings of yellow through it; a clear sign of infection.

With two sterling silver tools, he poked and prodded the wound for the other half of the bullet. The process seemed to go on forever. Fern began to lose hope when he pulled the metal piece from Poppy's side and tossed it onto the table beside the bed.

"Thank you," she breathed.

He raised an eyebrow and turned away from her.

"What now?" Gabe asked.

"I want to reapply the poultice before stitching her back up," Fern replied.

"That will not work. You will need to fetch leeches," Pete said.

"I beg your pardon?" she asked.

"I will place the leeches over the wound, and they will suck out the infection. It is called bloodletting, a process I'm sure you know nothing about."

She knew all about it and from the reading she'd done, the outcome was never great.

"No."

He swung around, coming within inches of her face. "You call me here to rescue your sister, and when I suggest a remedy to the problem you refuse?"

She shrunk away from him, her back knocking into Gabe's chest. He was behind her, supporting her on any decision she made. He trusted her. He believed she could save her sister. She inhaled, stood taller, forced her chin up and narrowed her eyes.

"I do not think that is a good remedy," she said between clenched teeth.

"I don't give a damn what you think. You, my dear, are not a doctor."

"No, I am not as you keep reminding me, but allowing the leeches to suck her blood when she is so sick is only going to make her worse."

"And how do you draw that conclusion when you weren't smart enough to search for any bullet fragments before sewing her up?"

His insult touched a nerve, and she winced.

"Hmmm?"

"Experience."

He eyed her.

"What experience would that be?"

"From working with my father. We should let the wound weep while I apply the poultice, and you can administer the proper medication."

He laughed. It was a loud guffaw laced with arrogance. "I am not going to stand here and listen to your assumptions of what *you* think should be done." He pushed Fern out of the way and walked toward Ivy sitting at the table. "Girl, go and fetch me four leeches from the river."

Ivy looked at Fern.

"Do not look at your sister. I am commanding you to do this."

"But—

"Do you want to save your sister?"

Ivy nodded.

"Then go!"

She leapt from the chair.

"Ivy, do not go anywhere," Fern said. "Sit back down." She turned toward Pete. "When will you give her some medicine?" It was the sole reason she'd wanted Gabe to bring him here. Poppy needed something more than what Fern could give her to work on the infection inside of her body even after the bullet was removed.

"I am not," he answered.

"Why?"

"I see no reason for it."

There were plenty of reasons, and just looking at Poppy was enough to determine a handful of them. Fern's lips thinned as she bit down hard enough to cause her jaw to ache.

"What will you do if the leeches don't work?"

He spared Poppy a glance while he rolled up the cuffs on his white shirt. "Let nature decide."

Fern stepped toward him. "You will do no such thing. If you have come here to prove a point, which I think is so, then you can roll down your sleeves and leave."

"You're an imbecile," he spat the words, "a derelict who cannot see that what you are doing is a hazard to those around you!"

Gabe didn't care much for Pete Miller and over the last hour he'd begun to despise the bastard. The man had it out for Fern. It didn't matter what she said or did, he'd find a way to make it negative.

He wanted nothing more than to run his fist into the man's flapping jaw, but he knew that wouldn't help the sick girl. The doctor would get what he had coming to him, and Gabe would be sure to be the one to deliver it.

"Please leave," Fern said, arms crossed over her chest.

Pete shrugged, walked to the door and picked up his satchel. "You should leave well enough alone, especially after what happened to your mother."

Fern straightened. Her eyes misted.

"What are you talking about?" Gabe asked, placing his hand on Fern's shoulder.

"She hasn't told you? I am not surprised." Pete looked at Fern. "It's a family secret isn't it?"

She leaned into Gabe, and he felt an overwhelming need to protect her.

"Doctor Montgomery poisoned his wife with doll's eye."

"Get out!" Fern screamed.

Ivy placed her hands over her ears as fat tears streamed down her cheeks.

"Think she's still innocent of the crime, Sheriff?" Pete asked.

He wasn't sure what to believe, but right now all he cared about was getting Pete Miller out of the cabin. He'd discuss what he'd just heard with Fern in private.

"You need to leave," he said.

"You'll be sorry. There isn't much left to do for the girl. You waited too long. The bullet has poisoned her blood, and she will die."

"You seem to expect that outcome," Gabe said, coming around Fern to face the other man.

"It is what I know. Being educated gives me that knowledge."

"I'd say experience is right along with education," Gabe retorted.

"Maybe, but in this circumstance no amount of experience Fern has, which is very little, will save her sister."

"Is it not your job to administer the proper care to those in need?"

Pete fixed the collar around his coat. "It is."

"Then give the girl the medicine."

"As I've said earlier, I see no need."

"Bullshit, Doc. The girl is ill. She needs all the help she can get."

"I've done all I can here."

"Have you seen Robby Fuller?" Gabe's question stopped Pete from walking out the door.

He shook his head.

"He hasn't come by to see his wife?"

"No."

"Seems odd since he's aware of what happened."

"I do not know the comings and goings of Robby Fuller."

"Why is it that you never asked how Poppy was shot, or who did it?"

"I was not concerned with the act, but merely the reaction," Pete stammered.

"Don't go far, Doc. I'll be stopping by soon," Gabe warned.

"I should bloody hope so. I cannot keep Sarah Fuller's body much longer."

"There is no need to. You can proceed with the burial."

Pete's pointy chin jutted out as he flexed his jaw. "Are you not bringing in Fern to look at her?"

"There's no need." He refused to give the man any more information. He was beginning to think the good old doctor wasn't saying all he knew either.

"I see." Without another word Pete took his leave.

Silence filled the room, and he turned toward Fern for instructions on what to do next. He'd wait to discuss the way her mother died until after they'd gotten Poppy on the mend.

Fern stood still, her arms listless. Her head tipped toward the floor. He was sure she hid her tears. Not one for emotions, he didn't show them, nor did he know what to do when others did, he ran his hand through his long dark hair.

Shit.

"I'm not leaving until she is well." He didn't know what else to say, how to convey he wanted to help.

She lifted her head, and her violet eyes glowed. The longer he stayed in Fern's presence the more his respect and admiration for her grew.

"You don't want to arrest me after what you just heard?"

"We can talk about that later. Right now we need to get your sister well."

"Thank you."

Poppy's thin body began to shake, and Fern went to her. He followed, feeling an uncontrollable need to protect the Montgomery girls. Together they bathed Poppy with the tepid water until she became lethargic again.

"Do you have a plan?" he asked.

"There has to be something I can give her. Something that will work similar to the medicine I wanted Pete to administer." She chewed on her bottom lip, a nervous habit he'd noted since being here.

She raced to the bookshelf on the wall opposite of them, and pulled a thick blue book from the ledge. She rifled through the pages, flipping them with enough force that she ripped one. Disregarding the torn sheet, she continued to scour the pages until she stopped. Her lips mouthed the words as she read silently. She slammed the book closed, and he followed her to the counter where she grabbed a stem with four white bulbs on it from the windowsill.

"What is that?"

"Garlic." She held it up to his nose and he made a face.

"That is some powerful stuff."

"Yes, and we are going to fill this cabin with its scent by the time we are done."

"What is its use?"

"It has many healing elements, and one of them is fighting infection. It is also used to flavor food."

"Great. Are we going to feed that to Poppy?"

"Yes, but I will need to peel and crush the garlic first, then I will cover it in honey, that way it will be easier for her to swallow." She pulled a white bulb from the stem and slammed it onto the counter. It broke into four teardrop shaped pieces. "Once the wound itself is cleaned I will use my crushed yarrow leaves to make a poultice and draw out the infection."

"And after we've done all of that?"

She paused to stare at him. "We pray."

Chapter Nine

It had been hours since they'd given Poppy the last strong dose of garlic. Fern brought the candle from the table to the bed stand and sat down. She'd need the extra light to place the poultice of crushed yarrow on Poppy's wound. It'd be the third one.

She wiped the cut down with warm water, and with sure fingers pressed the yarrow into the wound. The gash could no longer be open; and it was time to stitch the skin together. She pulled the thread from the whiskey bottle.

Drenched from the liquor, she strung the needle and began to meticulously sew the laceration. Minutes passed before she was done. Satisfied with the neat row of stitches, she went about mixing more yarrow with the beeswax. She pressed it together within her palm, mixing the ingredients together. When she was done, she lathered the stitches and skin, leaving it uncovered.

She sat back, unwound her hair from the braid and rubbed her tired scalp.

Ivy sat in the chair by the table asleep, a thick quilt wrapped around her small body. She was glad the girl had finally dozed off. She'd been worried about Poppy to the point where she'd been getting in Fern and Gabe's way as they tried to work.

The cabin was quiet, lit by the warm glow of a few candles, and she whispered a short prayer for her sister to get better. She clasped Poppy's hand in her own. The convulsions from her fever had gone, but it didn't mean the girl was out of the woods yet. Her skin was still red and warm. She refused to think what life would be like without her sister. The thought brought waves of nausea crawling up her throat, making it difficult to swallow.

She sighed, dunked the cloth into the basin of cool water, wrung it out and placed it on Poppy's forehead. Her own eyes heavy, she massaged them with her fingertips. She hadn't slept since yesterday, and her body was telling her she needed to rest. She flexed her shoulders and gave her head a little shake to wake herself. She couldn't relax until Poppy was out of danger.

Gabe eased through the door with an armload of logs. He went to the fireplace and carefully placed them on the floor so as not to wake Ivy.

"Thank you," she whispered, unsure if he'd heard her, but so tired she didn't have the energy to repeat it.

"How is she doing?" He nodded toward Poppy as he knelt beside the hearth to stoke the log with a metal poker before adding another piece of wood.

"The fever has come down a bit, but otherwise the same." She couldn't hide the distress in her voice.

"Do you have coffee here?"

"On the third shelf beside the sugar.

"How about a cup?"

"I don't drink coffee."

"Well, now is a good time to start."

He smiled, and her insides melted. She wasn't familiar with the emotions stirring inside of her when he was near, and she didn't care to explore them either. Poppy was ill and once she was better, he'd go back to accusing her of murder.

He rummaged through the cupboards until he found the tin labeled coffee.

She was a tea drinker, but she didn't care to tell him, and since he was making she'd not be picky. She smoothed the red hair from Poppy's cheeks, brushing it back with her fingers. *Please, God let her get well.*

He pulled a chair from the corner and sat beside her. His cheeks covered with the start of a beard, the black whiskers concealed most of the scar on the left side of his face. She wondered how he'd gotten such an awful injury.

"It'll take a bit for the grounds to sweat into the pot," he said, interrupting her thoughts.

She nodded.

"She will get better."

His words surprised her.

"I hope so."

"How long before we know if she's in the clear?"

She glanced at Poppy. "The next twenty four hours will tell us."

He nodded.

"I don't expect you to stay. I know you have other priorities."

He stared at her for a long while, his black eyes revealing honesty and something else she couldn't quite place. She pulled her gaze from his, drawn to him, to his scent, to his strength. His shirt sleeves were pushed up to his elbows, and she let herself imagine what his arms might feel like wrapped around her—protecting her from the outside world, from those who wanted to harm her. She yearned for his fingers to caress her, want her—love her. As quick as the fantasy came, she squashed it with the reality of what her life had become—of who she was and why any man might want her.

"I want to be here, Fern."

"You're the sheriff of Manchester, surely you have work to attend to."

"I've got a deputy to cover for me."

"You do?"

"Bill Holt, an old Texas Ranger." He gave her a sideways look. "How often do you go to town?"

"I like to keep to myself."

"Because of Mayor Smith?"

"He is one of the reasons, yes."

"I gathered you've turned him down a time or two?"

There was no need to answer him. Nothing seemed to get by him, and she guessed his inquisitive nature came with the job.

"How did you get the scar?" she asked.

She didn't miss the way his eye twitched, or how his jaw tensed.

"When I was twelve my family's homestead was

attacked by outlaws. The Drummond Gang was wanted in six states for armed robbery and murder. They killed my father, mother and older brother, Hank. My sister was in town at a friend's." He blew out a loud breath before continuing. "I was coming in from the fields. I saw them and was able to peg a few off, but I was young and they caught me. The leader, Charlie Drummond, took his knife to my face as payback for killing two of his men."

"Why didn't they kill you too?"

"I passed out from the pain." He shrugged. "Guess it took their fun away."

"I'm so sorry."

He averted his eyes from hers. "After I got well, I took my sister to my aunt's and hunted every last one of them down."

"Did you kill them?"

"Yes."

She didn't know what to say to ease the pain she'd seen in his eyes. She'd lost both her parents but not like he had. Her heart ached for the boy who had to witness such horror.

"It must've been awful." She reached for his hand.

His eyes met hers, holding her captive—raw, piercing, genuine.

She leaned into him.

He stood, went to the stove and poured two cups of coffee.

She spread out the wrinkles in her skirt, trying to collect herself and her unruly thoughts.

"Here you go." He handed her a cup.

"Thank you."

She took a slow sip and made a face. Not at all like her teas. The coffee was much bolder and very bitter.

"Putting sugar or milk in it may help with the flavoring," he suggested.

"I think I'll stick to tea."

He chuckled around his cup.

The sound caressed her soul. She longed for the companionship she'd seen within her mother and father's relationship.

"How did your mother die?"

She'd been waiting for it, the question he'd wanted to ask since Pete Miller left. All previous emotions disappeared, replaced with anxiety. Dread coated her skin in a sheen veil of moisture. There was nothing left to do but tell him the truth.

Not one for lies or false stories, she'd face his accusations, his doubts and pray he believed her to be a good honest person who had nothing to gain from poisoning a friend. If he didn't…she'd be crushed, not because she'd be tossed in jail, but because he did not trust her.

She inhaled, holding the breath within her lungs until it burned.

"She was given too much doll's eye during child birth." The words rushed out in one breath.

"Who gave it to her?"

Memories flooded her mind. Her mother writhing in pain, the baby stuck, lots of blood, her father desperate to save her.

"My father." She hung her head, but not before she saw the shocked look in his eyes.

"He was a doctor. Why would he poison his own wife?"

Her head shot up.

"He did not poison my mother. I told you earlier the root of the doll's eye can be boiled for a tea to help with childbirth, coughs and chest pains."

"How did she die then?"

She sighed.

"My father never used it before. He'd only read about the effects it had. He was flustered, and worried for my mother already. He would've tried anything. He didn't know how much to give, or what part of the plant was the most poisonous. If he didn't do something she was going to die." She closed her eyes;

seeing her mother slip away, the memory still haunted her. She swallowed past the regret and continued. "He gave her the white berries…she died within minutes."

"And the baby?"

"A boy, died inside the womb."

"He poisoned them both?"

She nodded.

"Son of a bitch," he whispered, surprised.

"He was distraught for weeks afterward. He refused to attend the funeral, he couldn't work, wouldn't eat. I took care of the girls and tried everything to make him come back to us."

"Did he?"

"No," she whispered. "After a few months he packed up everything, and we moved west. I don't think he knew where we were going. It was pure chance we ended up in Manchester and they needed a doctor."

"He was able to continue his practice here?"

"Somewhat. He was too preoccupied with finding out how poisonous the doll's eye was. He spent the two years after my mother died researching the effects the plant had."

"On people?"

"Goodness no." She went to the armoire beside

him, slid open a drawer and pulled a thick mass of papers tied together with twine. She handed them to him.

"What is this?"

"His journals."

"On the one plant?"

"Yes. He researched with mice and other rodents."

"It's how you know how much to give and what is the most potent part of the plant."

"Yes."

"Your father was very smart."

"It consumed him along with the alcohol."

"I'm sorry." He placed his hand on hers.

"I used to tell myself one more week of studying; one more bottle of whiskey and that would be it. He'd return, our loving, laughing father…but he never did."

"Sometimes we cannot change how losing a loved one affects us."

"I realize that, but we were here and he forgot about us." She couldn't help the anger in her voice.

"It must've been tough on you."

"I am not asking for your pity," she said, annoyed for allowing herself to lean on him.

"And I wasn't giving you any. I stated a fact. I bet it was damned hard."

She grabbed the cloth from Poppy's forehead, dunked it into the basin, wrung it out and ran it along the girl's arm.

"Is Pete from Boston?"

"He grew up here in Manchester." She continued to bathe her sister's skin with the cool cloth. "He came back from medical school shortly before my father passed away and opened up his practice in town."

"How did he know of your mother?"

"I don't know."

"Your father didn't confide in anyone that could've possibly told Pete?"

"My father never spoke of my mother after she died."

He frowned.

Once done, she dropped the cloth back into the basin, leaving it there for when she'd need to do the ritual all over again.

"Is it possible he might've had similar acquaintances in Boston as your father?"

"Yes, I suppose."

He nodded.

"There is something else." She folded her arms around her middle and squeezed. "A stem was pulled from the doll's eye in my garden room." She hadn't the time to think about how anyone knew of her doll's eye growing in the room off of the kitchen, or how someone could've gotten into her home and taken it. But that is exactly what had happened. When she checked on it this morning, a long stem was missing from the plant, pulled right from the root. She was baffled at who it could be. She wanted to question her sisters to learn if they'd seen anyone around their homestead while she was gone, but with Poppy ill and Ivy helpless with worry, she had to wait.

"When did you notice this?"

"This morning. I'd meant to ask the girls about it, but Poppy was shot, and well, you know the rest."

Gabe sat back in his chair, taking in what he'd just heard. All fingers pointed to Fern as the one who killed Sarah, but the ache at the base of his neck told him otherwise. If she'd done it, what was her purpose, and why would she tell him all of this? And if it was an accident, he believed she'd confess, unable to live with harming her friend.

The woman hadn't fired a single shot at Robby Fuller, who tried to kill Poppy. How was it she'd be able to poison another person, accidentally or not?

"You're sure you haven't told anyone of the doll's eye you grow?"

"The only ones who know are my sisters."

He took a drink of his now cold coffee. Pete Miller knew of the plant. He'd told Gabe of its whereabouts. Someone was lying. He didn't know if it was Fern or Pete. He wanted to trust Fern, but he couldn't excuse all the facts either. He rubbed his tired eyes. He'd need to piece this puzzle together. The only problem was there were too many missing pieces.

Chapter Ten

Gabe sat at his desk, his head lolled forward, and he propped a hand under his chin to keep from smashing his face onto his papers. He hadn't slept in almost two days and his body was suffering the consequences. He never fared well with little sleep, and he wasn't going to get any until tomorrow. It was his turn to guard the prisoners until the judge came through. The man was expected today but still hadn't shown up. He hoped it had nothing to do with Tommy's gang.

He hated to admit it, but he missed the coziness of Fern's cabin and the company that came with it.

Poppy's fever broke this morning and by late afternoon she'd woken, weak, but hungry as a bear after hibernation. He chuckled remembering the foul-mouthed girl and her demands. Poor Fern, she'd be running after the girl until she was well.

He couldn't stop thinking about his conversation with Fern. Someone had taken a piece of the poisonous plant. She didn't know who had stolen it, and denied any involvement, offering him little to go on. This left his inquiry into the murder at a standstill. Who was to blame? Whoever took the plant was aware of its lethal nature, that much he was sure of. What baffled him was the reasoning behind it all. Had this person intended to frame Fern, or to murder Sarah for their own benefit?

Bill walked into the office, bathed and shaved. "Thought you might be interested to know Robby Fuller is drinking at Hal's"

He grabbed his Stetson off the desk, slapped it on his head and headed toward the door. "Thanks."

"Need any back up?"

"No. I'll need you here if the judge comes through."

Bill nodded.

He hadn't seen Robby Fuller since before his wife's death. He hoped the spineless bastard would've stopped by Fern's while he was there, but the coward hadn't shown his face. One thing he was certain of; Robby was going to jail tonight for the attempted murder of Poppy Montgomery.

Gabe walked through the swinging doors of Hal's saloon. The clinking of glasses and low murmur of men's voices mingled with the occasional woman's squeal. Not one for liquor, he only visited the saloon to place order, or see Hal.

"Afternoon, Sheriff." Hal walked toward him, an empty bottle in each hand.

"How are things today?"

"Quiet, but I ain't complain'n."

The Saturday before Gabe had to wrestle Ralph Palmer to the ground. The farmer had drank too much whiskey and lost at cards. Looking around the place, he noticed that Hal had boarded up the shattered window, and removed the two broken tables.

"What can I help you with?"

"Lookin' for Robby Fuller."

"I heard what happened to his wife." He shook his head. "It's a shame. Talk is Doctor Montgomery's crazy daughter did it."

"Don't listen to everything you hear."

He spotted Robby leaned up against the bar, a glass of whiskey in his hand. He swayed to the left, then to the right, having a difficult time keeping his balance.

He tipped his hat to Hal and walked toward Robby.

"I've been looking for you," Gabe said.

The drunken man swiveled to face him and brought the smell of stale liquor with him. Gabe took a step back and inhaled the smoke filled room instead.

"What do you want?"

"You're under arrest for the attempted murder of Poppy Montgomery." He gripped the other man's arm and wrenched it behind his back.

"That bitch shot at me first."

"I have witnesses that say you fired first."

"Fern is a killer. She poisoned my Sarah." Robby's bloodshot eyes welled up with tears.

"Who told you that?"

"Doc Miller." The man struggled while Gabe escorted him out of the saloon and onto the wooden boardwalk.

"Your wife died from poisoning, but I'm sure the beatings you gave her didn't help."

"I never hit her hard."

"You broke one of her arms a few months back." He wanted to smash his nose, busting it into a dozen pieces. Instead he settled for yanking hard on Robby's arms. He was satisfied when the man hollered.

"She fell. I didn't do that."

"Yeah, right."

They left the front of the saloon and walked across the street. The sun beat down on them and intensified the smell coming from Robby. He marched him up the two steps and into the office.

"Well, that didn't take long." Bill held a cup of coffee halfway to his mouth.

"It helps when the bastard can't keep his own balance," he replied.

"I suppose it does." Bill hurried to open the heavy wooden door leading into the jail.

Gabe pulled the keys from his belt and unlocked the cell holding Ralph Palmer. The portly man didn't look too pleased with having to share his living quarters with the drunkard.

"Sorry, Ralph, you have a cellmate."

"How long until the judge comes through?" Ralph asked.

Gabe couldn't blame him for wanting to get home and back to his farm. He'd been locked up for three days. He studied the man.

"If you promise not to break the law again, and I get in writing that you will pay Hal back for the damages you caused at the saloon, I will let you go today."

Ralph jumped up from the stool he sat on.

"Sure thing."

"Bill will draw up the paperwork and then you'll be free to go."

"Thanks, Sheriff."

He nodded and shoved Robby into the cell, locking it behind him.

"You got nothin' on me, Sheriff," Robby snarled.

Gabe turned toward him. "I'd say the hole you shot into Poppy Montgomery's side is all I need."

"She should've shut her mouth."

"Is that your confession?"

Robby's face lost all color, and he narrowed his eyes. "Did I kill her?"

Gabe couldn't tell if he was hopeful he'd taken the girl's life, or if he was upset that he might not have. Either way the man made his stomach turn. Robby wasn't all there.

"No."

"Ha. Wish I would've and her witch of a sister too. She killed my Sarah."

"You sure it wasn't all the beatings you laid on her?"

"Go to hell!"

"Is that all you've got?"

Robby spat through the bars at him.

Gabe dashed his arm through the rods and grabbed

the man by the collar. He yanked him close, smashing his face into the metal poles. Blood dripped from his nostrils to mix with the sweat on his upper lip.

"I don't take kindly to being spit on. Don't do it again." He gave Robby a shove and walked away.

"Hey, Sheriff," Tommy Rainer whined from the other cell, "I need to piss."

"Use your pan," Gabe said.

"It's full."

"Piss in your damn pants." He closed the wooden door before sliding the two by four across and into the metal hangers.

"Damn you, Sheriff!" Tommy screamed. "Buzzards will feed off your carcass when I'm through with you. My men are comin'. You're no match for 'em either."

Gabe listened to the threat. He expected Tommy's gang to come. The outlaw was their leader, and they'd risk their lives to free him.

"You think he's right?" Bill asked from the desk.

"He's been locked up four times, and they've come for him each time." He poured himself a cup of coffee. "Can't see how this time will be any different."

Bill nodded.

"Where the hell is the damn judge?" He needed a verdict to hang Tommy. Without it he was a sitting duck, and the damn Rainer gang knew it.

"I'm beginning to think he ain't going to show."

"I hold the same sentiment."

Bill pulled his .45 from his belt and checked the bullets. "What's the plan?"

Gabe leaned against the wall. He didn't have one.

Chapter Eleven

"This tastes like cow shit."

"Poppy Montgomery, watch your tongue," Fern snapped throwing her hands into the soapy water to grab a dish and scrub it clean.

"Ah, hell. I'm tired of sippin' this broth. My stomach needs real food," Poppy whined from her bed.

"You cannot risk getting sick and tearing open those stitches."

"I'm not going to get sick. Just give me some damn vegetables and meat."

Fern wiped her wet hands on her apron and stared at her abrasive loud-mouthed sister.

"Poppy you're almost seventeen."

"What's that got to do with anythin'?"

"No beaus have come to call. Do you think it has anything to do with the vulgar way you speak?"

"There's nothin' wrong with how I speak. I say what it is I want to."

"That is the problem."

Poppy sat up straighter. Her bright blue eyes flashed with hot anger. "Why, because they can't take a strong willed woman? I am no different than you, Fern."

She laughed.

"We are plenty different, Poppy."

"You are independent and rely on no man. You work your garden and help those in need, not giving a damn what others think."

"You honestly believe I don't care what they think of me?"

"If you did, you'd stop all of this," she motioned to the garden room, "and act like a young lady wanting a husband."

Fern thought about what her sister had said. She had no gentleman callers, other than Mayor Smith, but she refused to consider him. It wasn't like she'd intended to portray an uppity mistress. She wanted all the things the other women had; a loving family and children of her own. Over the years of fighting for her freedom she'd built up a wall to ward off unwanted suitors. Men who didn't see things the way she did. In the process she'd exiled herself to this land and her garden—afraid to venture too far for fear of what she might encounter. For goodness sakes she went to Manchester less than a handful of times a year.

Poppy was right. She was no different than her sister. In fact, she was probably worse. She thought of Gabe, and her stomach fluttered. He'd never give her a second look. She was a gardener, an outcast, who had been accused of murder.

"You are right, and I'm sorry. I've taught you to be strong, independent, and although that may be a bad thing for husband fetching, it is a good thing when living on your own."

"To hell with what anyone thinks," Poppy said, and Fern knew her sister was just trying to cheer her.

"I'm not going to chase any of my suitors away," Ivy chimed in from the kitchen table.

"You've got a little bit of time yet, tart," Poppy replied.

"I think that's great, Ivy," Fern said, trying to encourage the girl. Two Montgomery spinsters were enough.

"I don't care what you say, I plan on marrying a wealthy farmer with lots of land," Ivy said.

"You should marry for love and nothing else," Fern told her.

"Love can be cruel, it's better to marry for money," Poppy grumbled.

"How would you know?" Fern asked.

Poppy's brows furrowed. She tossed the red hair from her face. "Ryan Young, that's how."

The young man who they bought their meat from? He was a good two years older than Poppy and lived with his Pa. They ran the cattle ranch a few miles north of their place. Fern searched her mind for any signs she might've missed that the rancher had courted Poppy.

"When did this take place?"

"The who's and what's aren't important…besides, it wasn't meant to be. Leave it at that."

Fern could see the sadness in Poppy's blue eyes and knew her sister was full of it. She cared for Ryan, but it was clear the feelings weren't returned.

"I'm sorry, Poppy. Why didn't you tell me?"

"There was nothin' to tell." A tear slipped past her lashes, and she wiped it away. "Marry for money, it will get you further," she said to Ivy.

Fern didn't reply, instead went to her sister, leaned down and placed a light kiss on her forehead. No words were exchanged. The sisters had a quiet understanding that had gotten them through many tough times.

A harsh knock shook the door and echoed throughout the room. She turned toward Poppy when she heard the click of a gun.

"Put that thing away," she scolded.

Poppy ignored Fern, holding her Colt .45 aimed at the door.

"Who's there?" she called.

"Mr. Davenport." The man's German accent was difficult to understand at most times, but today his voice seemed strained—weak.

"Now can you put the gun away?"

Poppy grumbled something Fern couldn't understand and placed the pistol under the blankets.

Once the gun was out of sight, she rushed to open the door.

"What can I help you with?" she asked, stepping aside so he could enter.

Ivy sat at the table working on her numbers and she decided to leave her there, instead leading Mr. Davenport to the two chairs by the fire.

He shook his grey head when she motioned for him to sit.

"Mine Angela ist zick."

It was odd he'd come to her at all since he'd made it quite clear he didn't believe in her way of thinking.

"Why haven't you gone to see Doctor Miller?"

"No time. You're closer."

Angela must be in a bad way if he'd risk her health to come here instead of going into town.

"What are her symptoms?"

"Chezt painz, dizziness," the old man said. His face wrinkled with worry.

"Let's head on over to your place. I will have a look at her."

He nodded.

She grabbed her bag and shawl.

"Poppy—"

"We'll be all right here. Go and help Angela," Poppy said.

She smiled and mouthed a thank you before closing the door behind them.

Chapter Twelve

Fern took one look at Angela and knew the young woman was in distress. Her pale complexion showed red blotches on her cheeks and neck. The hair around her face was damp, and her lips were a light shade of blue from her struggles to breathe. Fern grabbed a tongue compress from her bag and placed it in the girl's mouth to see if the airway was blocked. She couldn't see anything, which meant Angela wasn't choking, and there was something else ailing the young woman.

"Angela, can you hear me?"

Her eyelids fluttered at the same time her lips moved, but nothing came out.

"Mr. Davenport, when did she start to complain of chest pain?"

"She said she didn't feel vell ant vent to lie down, but fell to zee floor."

"When did all of this happen?"

"Hour go."

"Has she ingested anything unusual?"

He raised a grey eyebrow.

"Has she eaten anything different today?"

He shook his head.

She sighed.

"Well, why don't you tell me what she has eaten today?"

"Eggs zis mornink ant tea vit Mrs. Miller."

"When did Lucy Miller stop by?"

"A few hours go."

Fern's head shot up.

"Angela was fine before the visit?"

"Yes."

"How long after Mrs. Miller left did she complain of not feeling well?"

"A quarter pazt zee hour. Vat iz it?"

Fern didn't reply. Angela's symptoms could be from poisoning.

"You said they drank tea while they visited?"

"She offers it to all her friends ven dey come for visit."

"Do you mind if I have a look?"

"I vant you to fix mine girl!"

"I plan to, but I need to know what she drank in order to do so."

"Vat in hell does dat have to do vit anythink? She drinkz tea all of zee time." His voice vibrated off of the walls and ceiling.

"I'm sure she does."

She grabbed the two cups from the counter, both still half full with tea. She dumped them out carefully. One of the cups had something inside. Fern placed her finger into the cup to scoop it out. She gasped when she unraveled a small leaf from the doll's eye plant.

She ran over to Angela, pulled her up, and stuck her finger down the girl's throat until she vomited all over herself and the bed. Angela's breath had a sweet scent to it, a sure sign of poison.

Mr. Davenport screamed and fussed behind her, but she hadn't the time to explain. She placed her finger into Angela's mouth again, repeating the process until the girl's stomach was emptied. She gently laid Angela back down and made quick work of cleaning the mess, tossing the blankets into a heap on the floor.

Fern took a wet cloth and bathed the girl's skin, cleansing her of any more bile.

"Chest," Angela whispered.

"Does it hurt?" Fern asked.

The girl nodded.

She needed to give the girl something. She wasn't sure if Lucy had placed more than one leaf in Angela's tea causing a more severe reaction to the plant and possibly her heart to stop.

"I'll be right back," she said to Mr. Davenport before heading outside.

The afternoon sun was warm, but it didn't stop her from shivering. Her heart hammered inside her chest, and she was sure she could sprint across the field without getting tired.

She spotted the dandelions growing by the fence and ran toward them. She needed the root and was careful to dig up the soil around the yellow flowers before plucking them from the ground. Satisfied with the five she'd picked, she headed for the house.

A rider rode into the yard, and she recognized Gabe atop of his horse.

"How's Miss Davenport?"

How had he known she was here?

As if he'd read her mind, he answered, "Poppy told me where you were."

She nodded and kept walking. She hadn't the time to explain things to him. Angela was deathly ill. She prayed the dandelions would help with the chest pains and flush the rest of the poison from her insides.

She swung open the door.

"I need a small bowl and a pot of boiling water," she said to Mr. Davenport who was hunched over his daughter.

"I'll see to it," Gabe said to the old man and went to work looking through cupboards. He slapped a bowl on the counter beside her and lit the burner on the stove to boil the water. "What is the plan?"

"I'm gong to cut the root of these dandelions as thin as I possibly can. We will add a bit of hot water to make a paste, and I'll put it on her chest to help with the pains."

He nodded.

"Do not empty out the water after I've made the paste. I'll need it to steep the rest of the dandelion for her to drink."

"What will that do?"

"It will force her body to flush out any more impurities." She hesitated. "From the poison."

"Poison?" His dark eyes went wide.

"I'll explain later. Right now we need to save Angela's life."

They worked side by side for hours, feeding the girl the liquid, rubbing her chest with the salve and watching for any signs of distress. Fern was exhausted and laid her head in her hands. She sat on a chair, Gabe beside her. Mr. Davenport rested beside the bed where his daughter lay.

"When will we know if she's in the clear?" Gabe asked.

"From my father's research, if she hasn't succumbed to the poison by now, she is on the mend."

He nodded.

"How did you come to know she was poisoned?"

"The cups of tea." She pointed. To lift her arm sent a wave of pain up and down the limb. She'd overworked the muscle. "There was a doll's eye leaf in one of them."

"Who poisoned her?"

Fern turned toward him and met his eyes. "Lucy Miller."

Chapter Thirteen

"Angela, I need to ask you a few questions," Gabe said, pulling a chair close to the girl's bed.

She'd awakened two hours before, tired, groggy and unable to focus on anything for more than a few seconds. It wasn't until ten minutes ago that her sentences began to make sense, and Gabe felt he could talk with her to get some answers. Mr. Davenport had gone to check on his bees, and he wanted to utilize the time without the old man there.

Angela sat up slowly, and Fern positioned the pillow behind her back.

"Take your time," Fern said.

"Why was Lucy Miller here this morning?" Gabe asked.

"She came by to confront me about Doctor Miller," Angela said, her voice weak.

"Confront you about what?" Fern asked.

The girl sighed.

"He's been making passes at me for some time."

Gabe remembered seeing the girl at Pete's office earlier in the week.

"Were you two?"

"No, no we weren't. He is married, and I am not that type of woman," Angela insisted.

"But you liked the attention?" Gabe said.

She nodded and a tear danced down her cheek.

Fern handed her a handkerchief.

"I was flattered that was all, but Lucy didn't think it was right. She was tired of his wandering eye."

Gabe glanced at Fern.

"Do you know if Pete Miller and Sarah Fuller were together?"

She shook her head.

"Thank you for answering my questions." Gabe stood.

He made his way to the door, trying to piece all he'd heard together.

"Sheriff?" Angela called.

He turned to face her.

"Lucy mentioned there was another woman."

"Did she say who?"

"I'm sorry, she didn't."

He tipped his hat and exited the house. Fern's footsteps followed him outside. Darkness covered the land, and all he could see was her silhouette against the light from the cabin. He resisted the urge to reach out and caress her cheek.

"What are you going to do?" she asked.

"Head into to town and talk to Lucy Miller."

She placed her hand on his arm.

"Be careful," she whispered.

He couldn't see her face, but knew she stood directly in front of him. Things seemed to fit together when he was with her. He couldn't explain it. Fact was he didn't know if he cared to even try. All he was sure of was how he felt when he was with her. He stepped toward her, wrapped his arm around her waist, pulled her into his chest and planted his lips on hers.

The moment their mouths touched and Fern's lips moved with his, he knew there was no going back. Kissing her ignited a fire within him. Hot, feral need built in his chest, clawing its way to his arms, and he held her tighter to him. He wanted her and damn it he couldn't resist her any longer. He ran his tongue along her bottom lip before pulling away. He could hear her quick breaths as he set her away from him.

"I won't be apologizing, so don't ask," he said and left her standing in the dark.

Fern let the evening air cool her heated cheeks before going inside to check on Angela. Her fingertips brushed her lips. Gabe had kissed her. She hadn't stopped him either. She swept the wisps of hair from her forehead, unable to concentrate on anything but his arms around her. The chignon she'd wrapped her long dark hair in was loose and falling from the pins she'd used to fasten it.

Her restless behavior was to blame for the disheveled look. She tried to tell herself kissing Gabe was wrong, but every part of her denied it. She was a single woman, with wants and needs of her own, and being in his arms had felt so right.

She stared at Angela asleep in her bed, thankful the girl had pulled through and hadn't succumbed to the poisonous plant. The innocence she saw on the girl's face reminded her of Poppy. Anger pulsed through her veins for the broken heart Ryan Young had given her sister. He was a rascal with little regard for a woman's feelings, and she'd let him have it next time she saw him.

Fern picked up the cup with the doll's eye leaf in it. How had Lucy known of the poisonous plant? What puzzled her even more was how she'd gotten it from Fern's home. She searched her mind for a time when the doctor's wife had come to call and couldn't think of a single one. Someone must've given it to her, but who and more importantly why?

Chest heavy, and stomach unsettled, Fern took her leave when Mr. Davenport arrived. She hadn't thought to saddle Nelly when the old man had come by earlier and wasn't looking forward to the uncomfortable ride home. She flexed her thighs; the muscles were sore and her rump ached something awful. Reluctant to climb back up, her body felt like it'd been run over by a herd of stampeding cattle.

She blew out a long breath, hiked up her skirt and climbed on top of the horse. With a click of her tongue Nelly started off. She was grateful the bright moon lit the trail in front of her. Not one for traveling after dark, she squeezed her legs around Nelly's sides and gripped the lead.

Fern thought of the events that had led up to today. Sarah's passing and Angela Davenport's sickness, both poisoned by Lucy Miller. The mention of another woman, who Lucy had yet to poison, sent chills down Fern's back. She racked her brain for who it could be. Women were her only customers, and she thought of the ones who had come to see her recently.

She gasped.

Chapter Fourteen

Fern raced Nelly along the trail to town. The wind whipped at her hair, pulling it loose from the pins. The wild mane flew behind her. There was no time to stop and fix it, so she kept on riding.

She needed to tell Gabe about her conversation with May a few days before. She was sure the baby May carried was Pete Miller's. If what Angela said was true, she wasn't the only one who knew that.

She passed the church on the outskirts of town and galloped toward the sheriff's office. Skidding to a halt, she jumped from the horse and pushed on the door at the same time someone opened it. Fern flew inside, slamming into a hard chest.

"What the hell are you doing?" Gabe asked irritated.

She straightened, fixed her skirt, raised her hands to smooth her hair, but decided against it. There was no hope for her wild tresses so she didn't even try to fix them.

"I was looking for you," she panted.

"Well, here I am." He smirked, and her stomach fluttered.

"I know who the other woman is."

He waited.

"May Hansen. She came to see me the other day about getting rid of an unwanted pregnancy."

"Stay here." He left her to walk across the street.

She followed.

"You don't listen very well," he said without looking at her.

"I am not your wife. Therefore you cannot order me about."

"I am the sheriff and the law, therefore, I can."

"I highly doubt me following you is grounds for an arrest."

They came to Pete Miller's place, and he stopped before knocking on the door.

"Leave this to me."

She opened her mouth to argue, but he held up his hand to quiet her.

"Not one word, or I'll throw you in a cell with the other outlaws."

"You cannot—"

"Try me." He turned his back to her and knocked on the wooden door that was the Miller's home.

Lucy opened the door dressed in a soft orange colored chiffon dress, her blonde hair pinned back to hold the dozens of ringlets that hung down her back.

"Evening, Sheriff," she peered behind him at Fern, "Miss Montgomery. What can I help you with?"

"Is Pete home?" Gabe asked.

"He's in his office with a patient."

Gabe walked a few feet to the door adjacent to the one he was just standing at.

"We are not to bother him." Lucy hurried after him.

He ignored her.

She tugged on his arm.

"Pete said no one is to disturb him."

"I don't give a damn what Pete said." He opened the door without knocking.

Fern heard voices arguing in the other room, and she rushed to open the door.

May stood in the corner, her eyes big with unshed tears. Pete was a foot from her, a cloth in his hand, and Fern immediately smelled chloroform.

"I need to talk to you, Doc," Gabe said.

"What the hell are you doing here?" Pete swung around, a shocked look on his handsome face.

Fern glanced at May, trembling against the wall. She went to the other woman and placed an arm around her.

"Are you all right?"

The woman nodded.

She sent Gabe a concerned look.

"Care to explain what is going on here?" Gabe asked.

"None of your damn business, Sheriff." Pete pointed to Fern. "Why isn't she in jail?"

"Miss Montgomery is not responsible for Sarah's murder."

"Of course she is. She grows that blasted plant in her house, and might I remind you, she almost killed her own sister."

"Poppy is on the mend with no thanks to you, and Robby Fuller is sitting in one of my cells for shooting her."

"I couldn't do it, Fern. I tried. I couldn't," May said as she wept.

"I told you I'd take care of it." Pete left the conversation with Gabe to walk toward them.

"Stay right there, Doc," Gabe warned.

"I'll not be told what to do in my own place of business. Now get out!"

"PETE!" Lucy screamed. "Why do you keep doing this?" Her eyes lost all color, and her face turned a bright shade of red. "You've made me a fool."

Pete didn't know what to do. He swiveled toward Lucy then to May, his dark brows wrinkled. If it wasn't for his arrogant attitude and the way he'd treated Fern she might've felt sorry for him, but she couldn't dredge up one ounce of pity for the doctor.

"Why can't you just stop?" Tears soaked Lucy's face.

Pete went to his wife, and she shoved him away.

"Do not come near me!"

"Sweetheart, let's talk about this."

"She's one of them." Lucy pointed to May. "She's one of your whores."

"What are you talking about?" Pete asked.

"I came home during lunch one day. I heard you and Sarah Fuller in your office."

Pete hung his head.

"She was nothing—"

"You betrayed me over and over again. How many were there?"

Pete didn't answer.

"Did you ever love me?"

"I love you still," Pete said.

"I tried. I really tried to make you happy." She glanced at Fern. "You were so consumed with getting rid of her..." She shook her head. "Everything should've worked out...they'd all be gone and I'd have you back."

"Lucy, dear, what are you talking about?"

She stared blankly at him, before she pulled a gun from her skirt and aimed it at May. "You're just like the whores from the saloon. You seduced my Pete. He no longer touches me, or kisses me. He doesn't even look at me the way he used to. All because of Sarah, and Angela and you!"

"Mrs. Miller," Gabe warned.

"You took him from me," she shrieked.

Lucy needed to be distracted. Fern could think of no other way than to draw the woman's attention to her. "How did you get my doll's eye?" she asked.

"Doll's eye?" Pete's eyes filled with sadness when he realized Lucy had been the one who killed Sarah.

With the gun still aimed at May, Lucy smiled. "Your sister, Ivy, brought it into class for show and share day."

Ivy had known the plant was poisonous and must've thought it'd make a great discussion piece with her classmates. Fern couldn't be angry with her sister for not knowing her teacher would take the plant and use it to harm others.

"You must've known about this, Doc," Gabe interjected.

"Don't be absurd. I had nothing to do with Sarah's murder," Pete said.

"How'd you know about Doctor Montgomery?"

"I don't have to answer that. I sit on the council."

Gabe stepped toward him. His dark eyes bore into Pete. "Answer it."

"I wrote to Doctor Philips."

"Who the hell is he?"

"He is an acquaintance of mine, a doctor in Boston. I needed answers."

"No, you needed a reason to bully Fern and her sisters out of Manchester."

"What I do on my own time is none of your damn business, Sheriff."

"How did you know Fern grew doll's eye in her home?"

Pete was quiet. He glanced at his wife before hanging his head.

"Lucy told me that Ivy had brought the plant to school. I had no idea what she was planning."

Fern saw Lucy's face drop. Her eyes and mouth sagged downward. Without thinking, she pushed May to the ground as two shots went off. Her ears rang, and she tasted gunpowder on her tongue.

"Fern!" Gabe called.

She opened her eyes and saw Lucy lying on the floor across from them. Strong hands gripped her arms as Gabe helped her up. She pulled May to her feet.

Pete lay slumped over his desk, a single gunshot to the chest.

She glanced at Gabe.

"She shot him…and I had no choice but to fire." He wasn't boastful or proud. He was the law in Manchester and he'd done his job, but that didn't mean it hadn't come with some heartaches, and shooting a woman was now one of them.

She swung her arms around his neck, thankful he hadn't been injured.

He smiled down at her. "It's nice to know someone cares."

She did care, and hoped he could see it in the way she looked at him.

The shuffle beside them reminded her they weren't alone. May stood off to the side, a sad smile upon her full lips.

"Let's get you two home," Gabe said, his arm still around Fern's waist.

"What about them?" May asked just as Bill Holt came rushing through the door his gun drawn.

"Well, it's about bloody time you got here," Gabe said.

Bill could see there was no danger and holstered his gun.

"Damn it, boy, you ought to tell your deputy when things are goin' to the hogs."

"I didn't think this would be the result."

Bill nodded, went to say something, but stopped when he spotted May.

"I was just about to escort the ladies home," Gabe said.

Fern sensed Bill's attraction for the other woman and interceded.

"I am well enough to travel on my own. I only live a short distance from town, but perhaps Mr. Holt could escort May home?"

Gabe smiled.

"You mind?"

"Sure, thing…I…I'll meet ya out front." Bill spun around and went outside.

As they followed Bill, Fern grabbed May's hand.

"I will come by next week to check on you."

"I'd like that." May climbed up behind Bill. "Thank you, Sheriff."

Gabe tipped his hat. They watched until May and Bill disappeared into the darkness.

"I've got a few things I need to do. If you don't mind waitin' around I can take you home when I'm done."

She smiled, and he grabbed her hand, holding it gently within his own.

Chapter Fifteen

"Are you insane?" Fern asked.

"She is the only one I know, besides me and Bill, who can handle a gun well," Gabe said.

"I can do more than handle a gun, Sheriff," Poppy called from the bed.

"She is still mending. Robby shot her just four days ago."

"I know, but the Judge I was waitin' on was found dead west of Manchester this morning. Something tells me the Rainer gang is coming tonight, and I need back up."

"My sister is not going to be your back up, Gabe."

She arrived home late last night. He'd refused to let her make the trek alone. She had waited in town while he enlisted a disgruntled Mayor Smith to help him carry Pete and Lucy Miller's bodies to Adam Kincaid's, the furniture maker in town, to be fitted for coffins.

"Grab my Winchester, Ivy," Poppy said as she slowly got out of bed.

Fern raced to her sister. "No. You are not going to do this. I will not allow it."

"I am good with a gun, and he needs my help."

Determination enhanced her sapphire eyes, making them brighter. Fern knew she'd not win this argument.

"What if you're killed?"

Gabe stepped toward them. "She will be on Lou's roof and will remain there." It was a warning to Poppy and no one missed his tone. The girl had a reckless nature, and he'd picked up on it in the short time he'd known her.

"I'll stay there. I promise," Poppy said to Fern before disappearing behind the changing screen to dress.

She wrung her hands. How was she going to let her sister go? Poppy still had a hole in her side, and now she was being deputized to help capture the rest of the Rainer gang. Oh my, Fern was going to be sick. Black dots clouded her vision, and she sat down in the chair.

Chapter Sixteen

Gabe sat on the porch in front of his office. Tommy Rainer was locked in a cell at the back of the building. Gabe could still hear his screams. He'd taken all of Tommy's clothes, leaving him stark ass naked in the cell.

He snickered. He figured if the outlaws got the upper hand, he'd be able to buy some time while they searched for their leader's clothes.

He was sure the gang had killed the judge. When he'd been talking with Bill this morning, the outlaw bastard gloated that it'd been his men. Gabe couldn't beat him bloody, so he did the next best thing... ended the bastard's rant by taking his clothes. The son of a bitch wasn't so tough now, what with being naked as a newborn babe and all.

The seams of the old rocker whined as he moved it back and forth.

Tommy's gang was coming. He'd bet his badge they'd show before dark when the town was quiet and everyone had settled in for the evening. He glanced up and spotted the top of Poppy's Stetson. He prayed the girl was ready for what was coming. He made a promise to Fern he'd bring her sister back safe, and he planned on keeping it.

Bill was hunkered by a barrel behind the building in case the gang decided to ambush them from behind. He didn't think that would happen. The Rainer gang was all show and had the bull's balls to prove it. In each one of their robberies and breakouts they'd come straight into town without hiding their identities, taking what they wanted.

Killing came easy for the gang of rebels; they held not an ounce of remorse for the lives they took. Every lawman they came up against either died in a shootout, or was injured.

He didn't plan on being either.

He was ready for them. Earlier in the day he'd warned the shop owners and Mayor Smith of what was coming. No one wanted to have any part of the situation and agreed to stay clear of the main road. He wasn't surprised when none of Manchester's citizens volunteered to help him capture the gang, he almost expected it. The way they treated Fern was a clear indication of the kind of people that had settled in the town. Unfortunately, Mayor Smith and Pete Miller had influenced them.

Even with Pete gone, and his wife being the one who murdered Sarah, he didn't feel much would change in their view of Fern and her sisters. It was a shame. The Montgomery girls were kindhearted. He felt responsible for them. They'd come to fill the hole inside of him from the death of his own family. He never thought to find a place where he belonged, but within the cabin walls surrounded by all sorts of plants and herbs, he'd found a home.

The trampling of horse hooves brought his head up. They'd come early. He spotted the cloud of dust on the outskirts of town. His heart raced, but he held still. It took everything in him not to run out into the street and start firing.

Gabe glanced up at Poppy who nodded to signal that she'd seen them. He prayed Bill was ready. The riders came into sight. He counted five men on top of horses, hats low, bandanas covering their mouths and guns held high.

Gabe pulled his Colt from the holster around his waist and waited for the outlaws to get closer. Two shots rang out one after the other, and he watched surprised as two of the riders dropped to the ground. *Poppy.* He smiled. The girl was hell behind a barrel, and he'd underestimated her again.

The gang skidded to a halt, aimed their guns up to where Poppy was hiding and fired. He ran to the side of the building to shield himself and discharged his gun. Windows shattered, and the bullets hitting wood echoed around him. He fired again. One more outlaw hit the ground.

He aimed his gun when he heard a click behind him. Before he could spin around the gun went off. He dropped to his knees. His shoulder burned, and the gun slipped from his fingers. Damn it, he'd been shot.

His arm hung in an uncomfortable position. The shoulder drooped lower than the other. He could feel the warmth from the blood as it seeped from the wound. He had to get up. He had to protect Poppy. He couldn't let her face them alone. Where the hell was Bill?

Gunfire surrounded him. He hoped to hell some of it was coming from Bill and Poppy.

Another click.

He spotted his gun, a foot from him. He bit down hard until his jaw ached and lunged for his pistol. A loud bang followed by a thud sounded behind him. He turned. One of the Rainer gang lay dead, a hole blown into his side. Bill limped from behind the building; blood soaked the front of his denims. He'd taken a bullet to the left leg.

"Thanks," he said.

"The bastard came from the Mercantile. Must've come in from the south side of town."

"How many left?" he asked checking the chamber on his pistol for bullets.

"Two, but she's got it covered."

They glanced up at Poppy, hat down low, red hair flying behind her. She wielded two pistols and fired them at the outlaws. Gabe lifted his gun to help the girl, but was too late. The Rainer gang lay dead in the street.

Chapter Seventeen

Fern refused to look out the window another time. She couldn't see past the porch anyway. It was close to midnight, and Poppy and Gabe still hadn't come back. Maybe the Rainer gang hadn't shown, or maybe one of them was injured or possibly dead?

She stood and went about making tea. Keeping busy would take her mind off of what was happening in town. Ivy lay snuggled in Poppy's bed, fast asleep and snoring. She smiled. The girl was very bright. Today Fern had taken the time to talk and get to know her little sister better. While running the homestead and aiding those who were ill, she'd forgotten to sit and talk with Ivy, making it a priority now.

The girl worried she was responsible for Sarah's murder by taking the doll's eye to school. Fern reassured her that Mrs. Miller's actions were not caused by Ivy's innocence in being a child. In fact, her teacher took advantage of the girl, using her to do a despicable thing.

Ivy understood, and promised to never take anything from the garden room without asking Fern first.

The door slammed against the wall and Poppy walked through. With one arm around Bill, she helped him into the cabin. The deputy's leg was covered in dark blood. She made quick work of clearing her sideboard, and pulled it into the middle of the room. Fern pointed for Poppy to lay him on the long wooden table.

"Where is Gabe?" she asked, cutting off Bill's pant leg.

"He's takin' care of the horses," Poppy said.

"Thank God," she breathed. "I'm going to need some water and a clean rag."

Poppy nodded. When she returned Fern noticed the bucket was full of water.

"I didn't need that much," she said.

"Gabe's got a bullet in him too."

"Damn it, Poppy, why didn't you say so earlier?"

The bullet had struck in the fleshy part of Bill's thigh and didn't look to have hit anything major.

She'd need to remove it and make sure it was cleaned well. No infection would take his leg as she'd learned earlier from Poppy's injury.

"I need you to boil a pot of this water. Find the whiskey Pa used to drink as well."

Poppy rushed to do as Fern asked.

Her mind kept trailing to Gabe. How badly was he shot? Was he managing outside with the horses? She squeezed her eyes shut in an effort to concentrate on the task in front of her.

She'd mend Bill first then tend to Gabe.

Poppy returned with the whiskey and helped Bill drink it down. Removing the bullet was going to hurt like the blazes, and the alcohol would numb his body.

"Ready?" she asked Poppy, who placed her hands on Bill's shoulders.

The girl nodded.

Fern took the long silver tongs and held them above the wound. Saying a silent prayer for God to guide her hand, she took a deep breath, held it and dug the tongs into the hole.

Bill sat up and hollered.

"Hold him still."

"Damn it, I'm tryin'. The old bastard is strong."

Fern felt the pellet with the tip of the tong, and with steady hands pulled it from the bloody gash. She looked at the slug and blew a sigh of relief when she saw it was all in one piece. She'd not be digging for any fragments today.

"Let's get him cleaned and bandaged." She glanced at the door. Gabe still hadn't come in, and she worried something might've happened to him.

"How badly was Gabe wounded?"

"Shoulder."

She nodded.

Fern cleaned Bill's wound with warm water and a little bit of whiskey. She packed the hole full of yarrow and sewed it shut. She leaned back and wiped the sweat from her brow.

"This should do. Keep an eye on him. I'm going to find Gabe."

"You got it." Poppy saluted her.

Fern stepped out onto the porch. She was waiting for her eyes to adjust to the pitch black around her, when she noticed the light coming from the barn.

She pulled open the heavy door and saw him sitting shirtless on a stool by the lantern. Blood washed his back, and she could see the wound on the upper right side of his shoulder.

"What are you doing?" she asked, coming closer.

"Taking care of this," he said through gritted teeth. She came around him and was shocked to see he was stitching up the hole in the front of his shoulder. The bullet had gone straight through.

"Are you crazy? You'll get an infection." She took the needle and thread from him and finished the last stitch.

"I was doing just fine, thanks."

"I can see that. What were you using to clean this?"

He lifted up the bottle of whiskey and gave her a crooked smile.

"Well, it's best if you come inside so I can stitch the back." She reached for the whiskey and he grabbed her hand.

"We have a situation."

"Yes, and it involves the gash in your back that needs mending."

He shook his head.

She waited.

"It involves you and I."

She sucked in a breath. He'd not told her of his intentions toward her. She was sure of her feelings for him; just to look at him made her melt like butter on a warm July day.

He opened his mouth, but nothing came out, and his eyes moved from hers to the floor. Her heart sank. He didn't share the same feelings. It was to be expected, she was a spinster—an independent woman—and it'd become clear no man would see her as marriage material.

"There is nothing to say." She smiled. "Let's get you inside."

His head shot up.

"There is plenty to say." He ran his hand through his hair. "Damn it, I don't know how…I'm not good with words."

"Gabe—"

"Listen, I can't stop thinkin' about you. You're always in my mind and…well…"

"You don't like it?"

"Ah shit." He pulled Fern to him and pressed his lips to hers. With every caress of his tongue she felt his need for her. Gabe's hand moved up to the back of her head, pulling the pins from her bun as he held her to him.

"I want to kiss you for the rest of my life," he said against her lips.

"That makes two of us."

He smiled, and kissed her until the sun came up.

If you enjoyed this book, please consider writing a short review and posting it on your favorite review site. Reviews are very helpful to other readers and are greatly appreciated by authors, especially me. When you post a review, drop me an email and let me know and I may feature part of it on my blog/site. Thank you.

~ *Kat*